Josh Lanyon is the author of one previous Adrien English thriller, *Fatal Shadows*. He lives in California.

A Dangerous Thing

JOSH LANYON

Also by Josh Lanyon

Fatal Shadows

First published 2002 by GMP (Gay Men's Press),
PO Box 3220, Brighton BN2 5AU

GMP is an imprint of Millivres Prowler Limited,
part of the Millivres Prowler Group,
Worldwide House, 116-134 Bayham Street, London NW1 0BA

www.gaymenspress.co.uk

A CIP catalogue record for this book is available from the British Library

ISBN 1-902852-33-8

Printed and bound in Finland by WS Bookwell

Distributed in the UK and Europe by Airlift Book Company,
8 The Arena, Mollison Avenue,
Enfield, Middlesex EN3 7NJ
Telephone: 020 8804 0400
Distributed in North America by Consortium,
1045 Westgate Drive, St Paul, MN 55114-1065
Telephone: 1 800 283 3572
Distributed in Australia by Bulldog Books,
PO Box 300, Beaconsfield, NSW 2014

One

She was young and she was lovely and she was dead. Very dead.

And this was bad. Very bad.

What had once been Lavinia was now an ungraceful sprawl of long blonde hair and long white limbs – and then Jason's horrified brain recognised what his eyes had refused to see: Lavinia's slender arms ended in two bloody stumps.

I stopped typing, read it back and winced. Poor Jason. We had been stuck discovering Lavinia's body for the past two days and we still couldn't get it right.

I hit the delete key.

Lousy as was *Titus Andronicus*, my second Jason Leland mystery, *Death for a Deadly Deed*, was even worse. I guess basing Jason's second outing on Shakespeare's infamous play was only the first of my mistakes. I was still brooding when the phone rang.

"It's me," Jake said. "I can't make it tonight."

"It's okay," I said. "I wasn't expecting you."

Silence.

I let it stretch, which is not like me, being the civilised guy I am.

"Adrien?" Jake asked at last.

"Yo?"

"I'm a cop. It's who I am. It's what I do."

"You sound like the lead-in to a TV show." Before he could hit back, I added, "Don't sweat it, Jake. I'll find something else to do tonight."

Silence.

I realised I'd deleted too much from my manuscript. Was I supposed to hit Edit and then Undo? Or just Undo? Or Control + Z? Word Perfect, I am not.

"Have fun," Jake said pleasantly, and rang off.

"See ya," I muttered to the dial tone.

These dreary dumps I call my life.

For a moment I sat there staring at the blinking cursor on my screen. It occurred to me that I needed to make some changes – and not just in *Death for a Deadly Deed*.

I went downstairs to the shop where Angus, my assistant (and resident warlock), was slicing open a shipment of books with a utility knife.

"Angus, I'm going out of town," I announced as Angus gazed entranced at a best-selling cover featuring a blood-spattered axe.

I wasn't sure if I had a dial tone or not. He didn't blink. Angus is tall, rawboned and pale as a ghost. Jake has a number of unkind sobriquets for him, but the kid is smart and hardworking – I figure that's all that is my business.

"Why?" he mumbled at last.

"Because I haven't had a vacation in years. Because I can't write with all these distractions."

At last Angus tore his bespectacled gaze from the gory dust jacket. "Why?"

After a couple of months I was becoming fluent in Anguspeak.

"The way it is, man. Can you keep an eye on things?" Keep the Black Masses to a minimum and not eat all fifty boxes of gourmet cookies in the storeroom?

Angus shrugged. "I guess. Class starts back up in two weeks though."

I've never been able to ascertain exactly what Angus is studying at UCLA. Library Science or Demonology 101?

"I'll be back by then. I just want to get away for a few days."

"Where are you going?" This was the most interest in my actions Angus had shown in two months.

"I own property up north in Sonora. Actually outside of Sonora, near a little town called Basking. I thought I'd drive up there." I added, "Tonight."

"Tonight?"

"It's four-thirty now. It shouldn't take me more than six or seven hours."

Angus mulled this over, absently testing the point of the utility knife with his thumb.

"It's not like you to be impulsive, Adrien," was his verdict. "What do I tell that cop of yours?"

I said peevishly, "He's not my actual personal property. He's a public servant. Anyway you won't have to tell him anything, because I don't plan on seeing him anytime soon."

"Oh." Angus looked down at the knife with a small smile. Tiffs among the faggots were apparently the stuff of quiet merriment.

I left Angus with visions of dismemberment still dancing in his head and went to pack. It didn't take long to throw a pair of Levi's and a toothbrush in my Gladstone. I emptied the fridge into an ice chest, dug out my sleeping bag and tossed computer disks and a couple of CDs in with my clothes and laptop.

By a quarter after five I was fighting the workday traffic as I headed the Bronco out towards Magic Mountain and the 5 Freeway. Over the pass it was bumper to bumper, but what the hey, I had a thermos full of Gevalia Popayan coffee, Patty Griffin's

Flaming Red rocking on the CD player and I was heading out on an adventure.

Had I But Known, as they used to say in a certain school of mystery writing...

Outside Mojave, I pulled in for gas at a quaint filling station surrounded by Joshua trees and stacks of old tyres. An enormous purple gorilla balloon floated overhead as an advertising gimmick. I pumped gas and enjoyed an *Apocalypse Now* sunset while the giant balloon bobbed gently on the desert breeze. For some reason the grape ape reminded me of Jake.

Jake. If only it were as easy to leave the thought of Jake behind as it was to leave the city lights now twinkling in my rearview mirror.

Two months earlier Detective Jake Riordan had saved my life in what the papers unimaginatively called the 'Gay Slasher Killings.' When it was all over, Jake had received an official reprimand from the LAPD brass, and I had received an overture of sorts from Jake, a homosexual cop buried so deep in the closet he didn't know where to look for himself.

Riordan was tough and smart and handsome; and, other than that self-loathing hang-up, pretty much all I could have asked for in a potential mate. But gradually, little things, like the fact he couldn't bear to touch me, began to take their toll.

Okay, I exaggerate. He did put an arm around my shoulders once when we were watching a PBS documentary on hate crimes against gays, and he had taken to hugging me good-bye. It wasn't that Riordan was a virgin. Far from it. He was heavily into the S/M scene. But when it came to face-to-face, eye-to-eye, mouth-to-mouth, the Master turned into a schoolboy.

Witness our first and only necking session.

Riordan's mouth was a kiss away from my own when he gave a

strange laugh and pulled back.

"Shit. I can't do this." He ran a hand through his blond hair, looked at me sideways.

"Can't do what? Kiss me?"

He shook his head and then nodded.

"My mouthwash isn't working? What's the problem?"

Jake laughed but didn't answer.

"Why, Jake?" I asked quietly.

He blurted out, "I open my eyes and I see the pores of your skin – your skin's okay, don't take this wrong – but you've got five o'clock shadow. You smell like aftershave. Your lips –" He gestured briefly and hopelessly. "It's just – you're not a chick."

"You noticed." I sounded flippant but I was thinking hard. "So this is a new experience for you? You have sex with guys but you don't –"

"It's nothing like this," Jake interrupted. "This is like *dating*. This is... weird."

Yeah, and whips, chains, scourges and blindfolds were normal?

"I could let you tie me up and beat the shit out of me, but will you still respect me in the morning?"

"I don't want you that way," Riordan said. "I know you. It wouldn't be the same."

Swell. He preferred humiliating strange men in costume to kissing a man he knew.

"Let me get this straight. You don't want to have sex with me?"

"Obviously, I want to have sex with you."

Obviously. What was I thinking?

"But?"

Riordan said impatiently, "I don't know! Why don't we watch a video or something."

We watched a lot of videos. I became an expert on the films of

Steven Seagal. We went out to dinner a couple of times (though Riordan fretted some of his copper pals might spot him fraternising with a known homo). And we talked. No heart to hearts. Jake talked about his work and his family: mom, dad, two brothers (one in the Police Academy) all under the delusion that James Patrick Riordan was as straight as the proverbial arrow.

Mostly I listened; Jake occasionally asked me questions which I labeled under the general heading of 'gay lifestyle'. How many times a month did I have sex? When had I come out? Even though Jake was older and probably more experienced, I sometimes felt like his gay mentor or Fag Big Brother or something. A month of keeping company and then a month of excuses and cancelled engagements.

It was over before it began.

"Look," I told him one night when he arrived four hours late for dinner, "You're just going through the motions. Why bother?"

That tawny gaze lit on mine. Jake said bluntly, "I never meant to get involved with you, Adrien."

"Rest easy; you're not."

"Yeah, I am." And he put his big paw over mine.

Pathetic, but this is the kind of thing that kept me holding on. I use the term 'holding on' loosely, because for the most part life went on exactly as before, with the exception of the funny flutter my heart gave when I'd hear Riordan's voice on the other end of the phone – and for all I knew that was incipient heart failure.

It sure as hell wasn't love, because I refused to do something so self-destructive as love a man who hated himself for being homosexual (which, by extension, probably meant he subconsciously hated me, too). I reassured myself that although I liked Riordan, I wasn't closing any doors, wasn't missing out on any opportunities; I was still open to meeting new people, making new friends and lovers.

So why the frustration and anger, sure, even hurt, when the big guy pulled the plug as he had this evening?

Outside Bakersfield I made a pit stop at a rest area. I walked around and stretched my legs, bought a stale blueberry bagel from a catering truck and rechecked my *Thomas Guide* in the cab light of the jeep.

The full moon shone brightly, illuminating rolling hills dotted with oaks and occasional farmhouse lights. Miles of nothing but empty highway and starry skies. Miles of nothing but miles as I headed north with the big rigs once more. I was doing about seventy-five, kicked back on cruise control with nothing to do but think and remember.

It was twenty-four years since I had last seen my grandmother Anna's ranch. That was the summer before she died. I was eight years old, and summer vacations with Granna were the happiest times of my life.

Granna was kind of a family legend. One of those Roaring Twenties gals, she had left her husband and returned to her birthplace to raise horses and hell, as the mood took her. I remember her as tall, rail thin, with a silver bob and deeply tanned skin. My granny rolled her own cigarettes, rode like a bronco buster and swore in Italian – which was the language of her childhood nanny. It must have been some childhood, judging from the frequency and fluency of her swearing.

Anyway, there was no hint that particular summer that it was to be the last. But two weeks after I returned to my mother's fretting bosom, my grandmother had been killed in a fall from a horse. To my mother's chagrin, Granna had bequeathed her entire estate to me. True, Granna's estate was nothing to rival the fortune left in trust to Lisa, my mother, by my dear departed dad, but it was enough to ensure financial necessity would never tie me to Ma's apron strings.

I inherited half that money when I turned twenty-one, and I had spent it purchasing what was now Cloak and Dagger Books. I would inherit the balance when I turned forty, which around tax time seemed like a lifetime away. As for Pine Shadow Ranch, I'd had some furniture shipped down to me but had never gone back, preferring to remember it as it had been. There was a caretaker who kept an eye on the holdings, but for all I knew the place could have fallen to rack and ruin by the time I decided to take my 400-mile drive down memory lane.

It was nearly eleven by the time State Highway 49 had narrowed to pine trees and mountains. I cracked the window and the night air was startlingly cold and clean with the bite of distant snow.

I spent about eighty miles of winding road sandwiched between one of those monster trucks (high beams trained on my rearview) and a battered pickup with the license plate URUGLY. At five-mile intervals we would come to another blind curve and the monster truck would swing out in the opposite lane in a play-ful gambit of vehicular Russian Roulette. And thirty seconds later he would drop back into formation in time to avoid plowing into an oncoming car.

At last he made his big play, risked his all, and roared off around a bend, just missing a head-on with a logging truck. He vanished into the diesel-scented night.

Now it was just me and the 45-mile-an-hour wit in the pickup. Emptying the last of the Popayan coffee into my thermos cup, I fid-dled with the radio, trying to find a station that varied the thematic content of tears-in-the-beer, crying-on-the-shoulder-of-the-road, and hanging-on-to-nothing-but-the-wheel. Despite the caffeine overload, I was beat and my eyes felt ready to drop out of my head.

Fast approaching the stage of exhaustion where I wasn't sure if I was still driving or if I was only dreaming I was still driving, I nearly missed the turn-off. The next ten miles were a challenge to the Bronco's shocks as well as my own, but at last I recognised the landmark of Saddleback Mountain and knew the Pine Shadow Ranch lay right around the next bend.

I downshifted as we began our descent. The jeep rattled across a cattle guard. Ahead, the ranch lay motionless in the bright moonlight; from a distance it seemed untouched by time. Despite the dark windows and empty corrals I could almost convince myself that I was coming home, that someone waited to welcome me.

As I drew closer, I discerned the sign mounted on wooden posts above the open gate. Wood-burned letters had once spelled out, Pine Shadow Ranch. I slowed; the Bronco's high beams picked out a number of forms in the darkness: the barn behind the house, a windmill, a swing hanging from one of the trees – and something on the ground.

I braked. I was so wired I was willing to believe my eyes were playing tricks, but as I waited there, the Bronco's engine idling, the thing on the ground showed no sign of disappearing.

Too tired to be cautious, I climbed out of the jeep. It was no trick of light, no play of shadows. A man lay face down in the dirt.

I walked around him, my footsteps unnaturally loud in the clear night. From across the yard I could hear a broken shutter banging. The wind rustled the tall winter grass. I knelt down beside him in the headlights.

His face was turned to the side, so I could see his eyes were wide open, but he wasn't alive. His breath didn't cloud the cold air, his shoulders didn't rise and fall. There was a neat little hole the size of a quarter between his shoulder blades.

I sucked in my breath. This wasn't my first contact with murder, but I still got that sensation of watching from a separate solar system, which usually precedes passing out cold. It was like one of those party games where you have thirty seconds to memorise a dozen objects; inevitably you see details instead of the big picture.

The dead man looked to be in his sixties, maybe. His hair was thin, plastered to his head. He was grizzled and his fingernails were dirty. He wore faded jeans, a plaid flannel shirt and cowboy boots. I had never seen him before, or if I had I didn't recognise him.

Reaching out to touch his wrist, a shock rippled through me like I had not been properly grounded.

He was still warm.

I jerked my head up and stared at the silent house. I looked to the surrounding hills, the sentinel trees.

The wind whispered in the pines. Otherwise, nothing moved. All was still. In fact, too still.

Staring into the windswept darkness I became convinced someone was out there watching me. The hair prickled at the nape of my neck. My heart began to give my ribs the old one-two; a left and a right and then a left left left.

I don't have time for this, I warned my uncooperative ticker as I slammed back into the Bronco. I reversed in a wide arc and put the pedal to the metal, bumping and banging down the pot hole-riddled road back the way I had come.

While I bounced along the road I felt around for my cellphone. I found it at last and dialed emergency.

It took a while, but I got through to a sleepy someone in the sheriff's department who finally seemed to understand what I was squawking about and promised to send help.

True to her word, the dispatcher did send the cavalry. A black and white four-wheel drive met me at the mouth of Stagecoach Road twenty minutes later, lights flashing, siren blaring.

"What seems to be the trouble, sir?" The man in uniform was middle-aged, well-fed and a different species from the cops I'd come to know in the past few months.

I explained what the trouble was.

"Okay dokey," said Sheriff Billingsly, scratching his skunk-striped beard. "You hop in the truck and we'll go have a looksee at this alleged dead man."

I piled in the cab with the sheriff and his waiting deputy, who was introduced to me as 'Dwayne.' Dwayne looked like he had just walked off the set of *The Dukes of Hazzard*. He shifted his chaw to his other cheek.

"Howdy."

"Hi," I said through teeth starting to chatter with cold and nerves.

Dwayne put the truck in gear and we headed back down the road.

"It was up here," I said as we clattered over the cattle guard. "Just outside the gate."

"Right along here?" the deputy asked, slowing as we approached the gate. The headlights fell on empty dirt road.

"Stop," I ordered. "It was along here that I found him."

The deputy braked hard and the three of us lurched forward and then back.

"Here?" the sheriff demanded.

The three of us stared at the lone tumbleweed somersaulting across the deserted yard.

"He was right there," I said.

Silence.

"Well, he ain't there now," said the sheriff.

Two

I awoke after a long, dreamless sleep. Slowly my vision focused on two beady eyes gazing into my own. A squirrel stood inches from my nose, whiskers twitching in alarm.

The alarm was mutual. I sat up yelling and swung the makeshift pillow of my jacket at my bedmate. The squirrel took off in a cloud of newly disturbed dust and disappeared up the chimney of the fireplace at the far end of the room. Coughing, I staggered to my feet and looked about.

Layers of velvety dust covered everything not draped in sheets. Chairs, tables, most everything was covered in dust sheets. It was like waking up in the middle of a ghosts' tea party. Cobwebs were draped artistically from the blackened ceiling beams.

Last night when I finally collapsed on the overstuffed sofa, I had been too frazzled and exhausted to notice. Today it was clear to me that I'd had some kind of breakdown. Only a lapse of sanity could explain what I was doing shivering in my skivvies in a room that time forgot.

April is plenty cold in the mountains despite the sunshine and wildflowers. I pulled on Levi's. In honor of Jake I fished a beer out of the cooler and swished a mouthful through my teeth as I sat on the ice chest lid and considered my surroundings.

This room was long and wide with a huge stone fireplace at one end. The wooden floors were bare now but in Granna's day they had been covered by starkly beautiful Indian rugs. As I recalled, the sheets concealed dark and heavy Victorian furniture, black walnut upholstered in red velvet or smoky-gray tufted satin. Heavy drapes framed picture windows and a view that was worth framing. Beyond the trees, in the distance, I could see mountains, still white-tipped with snow. The sky was cerulean – a word we don't use much in LA. Not a cloud, not a plane, not a telephone wire to mar that wide blue yonder.

The silence seemed unnatural and would take some getting used to. I heard the sweet trill of a meadow lark, then nothing else. No distant roar of traffic, no voices. Pure silence. I listened to it for some time, waiting for something to break the spell.

Nothing.

Then, lubricated by another swig of beer, the wheels began to turn. Already the events of the night before felt like some half-forgotten nightmare – much the conclusion local law enforcement had come to after they were unable to find any trace of 'my' dead body.

"Probably just the way the shadows fall here," the sheriff had said generously, not giving in to what was clearly his suspicious first thought.

"I'm telling you, it was a body."

"Coyote maybe," Deputy Dwayne suggested. "Could have been shot by a rancher and maybe dragged itself off to the hills."

"There you go," the sheriff said promptly, pleased with this scenario.

"It was not an animal," I said. "I got out and knelt beside it. It was a man." I described the man to them for the second time.

"Could be Harvey," the deputy said reluctantly, with a look to his superior.

"Sure, drunk again. Or maybe stoned," the sheriff agreed. "I guess that's possible."

"Ted Harvey? The overseer?"

"*Overseer?*" repeated the sheriff. He and the deputy exchanged glances. "Sure that's it. Probably came to and staggered on home to sleep it off."

"Probably puking his guts out right now," the deputy comforted and shot a stream of tobacco juice at a mustard flower swaying in the night.

I was shaking my head, and the sheriff said shortly, "Sir, I believe you think you saw something this evening. I don't think you are deliberately wasting taxpayer money and tying up government officials for nothing..."

Call me paranoid but I sensed an implicit threat. "But?" I asked.

"But you can see for yourself there's nothing here. No blood. No body imprint in the sand."

"There goes the coyote theory."

They both looked at me without favour.

"Whatever it was, it's gone now," Sheriff Billingsly said. "Not much we can do about that. Moon's setting. It'll be black as a nigger in a coal mine in half hour."

Charming.

I said, "You could check to see if Harvey made it home. He lives on the property in a trailer, I think."

"Sir, I don't have the authorisation to waste any more time on this. There's nothing *here*."

So sayeth The Law.

They drove me back to the Bronco, advising me to head into Basking and get a room for the night at a motel. Charged to "Drive safe now," I was left yawning with nervous exhaustion in the glow of their tail-lights.

Ready to die with weariness, I drove creepingly back down to the ranch, scanning the side of the road for my missing corpse as though we could have somehow missed it. At the ranch I unlocked the front door, unloaded my gear and crashed on the nearest sofa. If the missing dead body had been propped in one of the chairs I wouldn't have noticed.

Eight hours later I woke a little stiff, a little uneasy but almost willing to believe I had been delirious with tiredness the night before. Almost.

Yet sitting there in the spring sunshine, I felt oddly calm. Maybe it was the change of scenery. Maybe I was still too tired to feel much of anything.

I studied the room. Really, apart from the coating of dust and cobwebs, things weren't too bad; nothing a mop and a bucket of disinfectant couldn't put right. Mousetraps were definitely in order, and I seemed to recall my grandmother saying that a small snake could get in anywhere a mouse could.

Lord of all I surveyed, I sat on the ice chest and considered whether I had any responsibility to pursue the riddle of the riddled corpse. I had called the cops and they had investigated and dismissed the idea of foul play. So that was it, right? Case closed.

Flapping into a shirt I headed outside to the trailer parked back behind the empty corrals. There was a battered white pickup, which I took to be Harvey's, beside the trailer. I felt the hood. Cold.

I banged on the rusting door of the trailer.

From inside I heard someone speaking, urging quiet.

"Hey! Anybody home?"

The whispering went on.

I tried the door. It opened.

I poked my head inside.

It only took a glance to ascertain the cautioning voice came from the television. An episode of *Bassmasters*. Ted Harvey might be living here – it smelled like he had died here – but there was no sign of him now. There was plenty of evidence he led a rich and full life, if the stacks of *Playboy*, empty beer cans and dirty dishes were anything to go by.

Walking the length of the trailer, I half-expected a body to fall from the closet or slump out of the cupboard-size shower. But dead or alive, nobody was home. I glanced around for a picture of Ted; there was nothing in the way of convenient snapshots. I turned off the TV, clicked off the still-burning lights. The lamps must have been on when I arrived the night before, but I had been past noticing. I didn't know what the cops would make of it; blazing lights and blaring TV indicated to me that Harvey had left after dark and unexpectedly.

I stood there for a few moments staring out the 2 x 4 window at green hills with patches of snow that were really white wild flowers. I asked myself what Grace Latham, would do – Grace being the sleuth creation of Leslie Ford, my favourite mystery writer. I guessed that Grace, in my position, would have done a little discreet snooping through Harvey's personal belongings. Grace's snooping usually led to Grace getting knocked over the head.

I backed out, shut the door again.

Even if my eyes had been playing tricks on me last night, and I had mistaken a man dead-drunk for a man dead-dead, the drunk had not picked himself up and staggered home.

I retreated to the house.

In the kitchen I boiled a few dishes, scoured the stove and mahogany table, fried up some turkey bacon and the only two eggs that had survived the road trip, and made my plans while I ate.

For the record, my plans had nothing to do with sleuthing, and everything to do with writing. I'd had enough sleuthing recently to last me a lifetime.

The new year got off to a helluva start with the murder of one of my oldest and closest friends. For a while it had looked like, if I didn't actually end up a corpse myself, I would spend the next twenty years playing touch-tag in prison with guys who had nicknames like Ice Pick and Snake.

But that was all in the past. I was done with a life of crime – except the fictional kind. My own first mystery *Murder Will Out*, featuring gay sleuth and Shakespearean actor Jason Leland, was now only months away from publication. I was hammering out the sequel in between bouts of writer's block.

The funny thing is that I never suffered from writer's block until I actually sold a manuscript. That's when the creative paralysis first set in.

"You're probably thinking about it too much," Jake commented in one of those irritatingly perceptive moments that make him a good detective.

After breakfast I got back into the jeep and drove to Basking to pick up some supplies; not that fried eggs and beer for breakfast didn't make me feel macho as hell, but as a steady diet it gets old fast.

Basking is much smaller than Sonora, which is one of the better known of California's old mining towns, as well as being the County Seat. This is Mother Lode country, but nowadays revenue comes from logging, tourism and agriculture. Mark Twain and Brett Harte made this area famous, but the tourists have yet to zero in on Basking. It's a small town; some buildings date back to the 1800s, which is old in California. The narrow, steep streets are partially bricked and lined with trees older than the town itself. Glass front windows painted in old-fashioned script spelled things like: *Gentlemen's Haberdashery* or *Polly's Confectionery*. Victorian clapboard houses have been preserved to dollhouse perfection in kindergarten colours.

There were few people about on that Friday morning; a couple of geezers sat outside the grocery store as I climbed the wide wooden stairs to the porch.

"So Custer says to his brother," one of the old geezers said to the other, "I don't know what the hell's wrong with them Injuns – they seemed okay at the dance last night!"

The second old-timer cackled in toothless appreciation and slapped his knee.

The bell rung noisily as I stepped inside the store. The first thing that met my eyes was a gigantic moth-eaten buffalo head mounted over the counter. My gaze dropped to meet that of a lady of about eighty (give or take a decade) calmly eyeing me as she picked her teeth with a blue toothpick.

"Help you, sonny? You look lost."

I told her what I needed and she directed me amiably down the aisles of pickled calves feet and pork rinds.

"Do you sell Tab?"

"Sonny, I haven't seen that stuff since the sixties."

"Passing through?" she inquired around the toothpick when I piled my groceries on the counter at last.

"No. I'm staying out on Stagecoach Road."

She eyed me with her gimlet eyes and gave an unexpected cackle that I thought would end with her swallowing her toothpick. "I know you now. You're that skinny little kid used to come in here with Anna English."

"That's me."

She removed the toothpick and waved it at me to make her

point. "Grandkid or something, ain't you? Only living kin. You're the one paying that no account Ted Harvey to sit around and smoke dope all day."

"I'm paying him to look after my property." Smoking dope was a perk.

"That's what you think, sonny," the crone informed me. She began to ring my groceries on an antique register, raising her penciled-in brows at such oddities as smoked almonds and apple-cinnamon instant oatmeal.

"Planning to stay a while, I guess," she remarked.

"A week or so."

"You got company with you?"

"No." I said it and immediately thought better of it. "Not until tonight." Why advertise that I was by myself in an isolated valley?

"How come you never came back when your granny passed away?"

"I was eight. I didn't have my driver's licence."

This reminded her of all the people who did have licences and shouldn't. She treated me to a couple of traffic-death horror stories, finished bagging my groceries and remarked, "You better have a pow-wow with that no account Ted Harvey. He'll burn the place down one of these days."

When I got back to the ranch I had another look for that no account Ted Harvey, but he was still missing.

The rest of the afternoon I spent making myself at home, home on the range. I threw open the windows and doors to air out the place, I balled up the dustsheets and attacked the most noticeable cobwebs with a broom that looked like a collectible itself. I dusted, scrubbed, swept – anything to avoid writing. However, the war machine ground to a halt when I reached my grandmother's study.

There, long forgotten by me, were several glass front bookcases loaded with books.

I approached slowly, my pulse quickening in excitement known only to book lovers in the advanced stage of addiction. Wiping the dusty pane, I peered close, and there before me in white print on black cloth were the words, *The Bride Wore Black*. Cornell Woolrich. Mysteries.

I expelled a long breath. Hundreds of mysteries. Paperback and hardcover. Agatha Christie and Raymond Chandler. All the good old stuff: Hammett, Tey, Stout, Marsh – and my fave rave, Leslie Ford. Young Jim Hawkins couldn't have been more jazzed at a trunkful of pirate gold.

No gay mysteries, of course. The first 'normal' gay detective didn't come out, literally speaking, till 1970 with Joseph Hansen's *Fadeout*. Hansen may not have hit the *NY Times* Bestseller List with his Brandstetter series, but he set the standard for the rest of us.

About five o'clock I tore my nose out of the books long enough to cook up and scarf down salmon fried with potatoes just the way Granna had taught me twenty years before.

After supper, I popped Andrea Bocelli into the CD player. I found a couple of hoary logs in the wood carrier, tossed them in the fireplace and curled up with one of Ford's Grace Latham mysteries. Grace is the quintessential amateur sleuth of her Post-WWII era. She's wealthy, well-bred and usually way off the mark in her detecting, so don't ask why I feel kinship with her.

Several blissful hours passed before my concentration was disturbed by the distant grind of a truck engine.

I wandered outside on to the deck which went clear around the house. In the distance I could see headlights moving down the mountainside like spectral lights. That road was the old stagecoach road and it led to this house which had originally been the old stage stop. Shoving my hands in my pockets, I waited. The night smelled of wood smoke and the roses growing wild beside the house. It was cold. I longed for the warmth of the house wafting out through the open door.

As I stood there rocking back and forth on my heels I began to feel very much alone, miles from town, miles from the nearest neighboring ranch, miles from nowhere. The wind through the trees sounded like rushing water, a mournful sound. It was a quarter of a century since I'd been out of hailing distance of other people. *City boy*, I jeered myself.

After a time, the sound of the engine died away with the lights. That was weird. Were they camping in the woods?

Rustlers, suggested my mystery-saturated brain. Slim pickings for rustlers these days. Briefly, I thought about investigating. Perhaps here lay the answer to my missing corpse. But unlike my intrepid Jason – or even good old Grace Latham – I had to conclude that night reconnaissance was not such a hot idea. Even more briefly I considered calling the sheriffs, but after our last encounter I hesitated to look like the nervous nellie I knew they had pegged me for.

Going back inside, I threw a couple of logs on the fire and returned to my book. But shortly, the lines began to run together, and worn out by more physical activity than I'd had in a month, I crawled into my sleeping bag and fell instantly asleep.

I woke to the hoot of an owl. For a moment I wondered where I was. It was dark in the room. The shadow of a tree swayed against the wall. Lying there squinting at the red embers in the fireplace, I listened intently.

At last I heard it, the crunch of footsteps on gravel. I rolled out of the sleeping bag and went to the windows. The night looked like it had been shot through a blue filter for a cheap horror flick.

All was silent. Still.

Had I imagined it?

Pulling on a pair of jeans, I shoved my feet into shoes and grabbed my flashlight. The air was bitterly cold as I stepped out on to the deck. The surrounding mountains prickled with gleaming arrowheads of pine. Walking along the deck, I paused as a wooden board cracked underfoot as loudly as a bone break.

I lingered but nothing moved.

I continued on around the house.

The outlying sheds and barn stood dark and motionless in the moonlight. Frost glittered on the rooftops. Quietly, I picked my way down the steps. Nothing stirred in the yard. It felt like hours passed while I watched and waited. I was tired. I was cold. I told myself that if there had been a prowler, he was long gone now. I reminded myself that I was a writer, not a detective, amateur or otherwise, and not constructed for such adventures.

Finally I gave it up and headed back inside the house. I tossed another log on to the dying embers in the fireplace. Diving for the sofa, I shivered into my sleeping bag.

After a few minutes my body defrosted and I sank back into confused dreams of Grace Latham sweeping cobwebs out of Ted Harvey's trailer.

We've got to get to the bottom of it, she informed me in my dream-state.

The bottom of what?

The floor, Grace replied simply.

I was up with the birds, a meadow lark providing a pleasant substitute for my alarm clock. In the chilly first light, I wandered past the empty corrals, the empty stable and the empty trailer of my missing handyman, then up into the hills.

I roved out quite a way, enjoying the warm kiss of sunlight on my face. Taking my time I climbed the hillside, which was really more of a small mountain. 'Find the nearest mountain, climb it, and peace shall flow into you as the sun flows into the trees,' said John Muir. At the crest of the hill I paused and inhaled a lungful of mountain air. When I stopped coughing I looked around.

That's when I noticed the field I was standing in was not of wild flowers, nor wild grasses nor bracken, familiar though those ragged green leaves seemed.

Running it through the old calculator, I deduced that I was waist high in grass – the kind you smoke, not mow. For a moment or two I stood there quietly aghast and then I tore down the hillside and into the house to the telephone. (I knew there was a reason I continued paying for the service.) I called my old pal Detective Jake Riordan.

Drumming my fingers on the scratched counter, I waited for the answering machine. After four rings Jake picked up and mumbled, " 'Lo?"

"Jake," I gasped, still puffing from my run. "It's me. I need hel– advice. When I got here there was a body – a dead man in the yard. He'd been shot. In the back. When the sheriff got here he was gone. Vanished. Now I've just found grass – pot growing on my hill."

Into my pause for breath Jake growled, "How the hell much coffee have you had this morning?"

In the background I heard a voice murmuring inquiry. A feminine voice.

I don't know why it hadn't occurred to me until then that Jake was still seeing other people. Female people. I figured he was still doing the leatherscene; I accepted that as a normal part of his screwed-up psyche. But dating women? Sleeping with women?

Where exactly *did* I fit in his life? Apparently he could sleep with everyone but me. Friends? I was the friend he didn't want to be seen with. So if we weren't friends and we sure as hell weren't lovers, why was I placing hysterical phone calls to him on a Saturday morning before breakfast?

"Never mind," I said. "Wrong number."

"*Adrien*, where –"

I replaced the receiver quietly and carefully, not slamming it down because I was an adult after all, and whatever I was feeling now was my problem, not Jake's. But the unrequited gig was getting old fast.

I wandered into the front room. It was way too quiet. I punched Play on the CD player and stared out the window. There's a phrase in *Titus Andronicus*: 'the heart's deep languor.' For the record, it wasn't that I didn't understand. And it's not that I don't like women. Some of my best friends are women. Women intrigue me with their fragile little bones and Amazon loyalty. I dig their Junior Scientist makeup kits, their Machiavellian reasoning, their extraordinary notions of nutrition and geography. I just wouldn't want my son to marry one. Okay, maybe my son, but not my boyfriend.

Spooky footfalls in the night are not nearly as frightening as the prospect of being alone and lonely.

One of life's little ironic moments occurred then as the next CD dropped on the player. *Con Te Partiro*: Time to Say Goodbye.

Three

My first instinct had been to yell for help. As that was a scrub, I swung my sights towards a more realistic solution for my mounting problems.

No doubt your standard issue solid citizen would have promptly summoned Sheriff Billingsly and his tobacco-spewing sidekick. But previous experiences with the local law had impressed upon me the awe-inspiring dearth of imagination there. I started remembering search and seizure horror stories where innocent landowners had their property confiscated by the state because of dope-dealing tenants and guests.

On the other hand, I couldn't simply ignore the fact that I had hashish growing on the North Forty. Not the easiest thing in the world to conceal either. I considered a controlled burn and briefly dwelt on the mental picture of my stoned woodland friends falling out of trees and sky. Uh uh, as my erstwhile pal Riordan would have said.

What I needed was some legal advice, so I placed a long distance call to dear old Mr Gracen, the last surviving partner of the illustrious firm of Hitchcock & Gracen. It being Saturday, my legal advisor was not in. The receptionist asked if it were an emergency? I said I wasn't sure, left my number, and resumed my nervous pacing.

After a couple of miles up and down the oak floors, I realised I was as aggravated over what I was not letting myself think about (Jake), as I was over the marijuana. Since I couldn't do anything about either at the moment, it seemed pointless to go on worrying. I told myself this several times.

Impelled by the kind of horrible fascination that draws people to the scenes of accidents, I scaled the hill once more and studied my former caretaker's vision of God's Little Acre. If Ted Harvey had planted this cash crop I didn't believe he would willingly walk away, so either he was due back shortly or he was my now-you-see-him-now-you-don't dead man. Vaguely, I considered drug deals gone wrong. Surely that kind of thing happened *after* the harvest?

As I stood there fretting and fuming, I noticed a wisp of white smoke drifting from the valley on the other side of the mountain. Spaniard's Hollow. I'd forgotten the local legend if I ever knew it, but I remembered that on the steep vertical rocks above the glen were petroglyphs, Indian symbols carved into stone. Way back in the days before the stage stop had been built, even before the gold-miners had arrived, the Kuksu, a secret Indian society used to hold religious ceremonies in these hills. In the hills and in the dark caves hidden in their shadows.

Naturally, I was curious. For one thing, Spaniard's Hollow is still part of Pine Shadow property, not a campground.

I started down the uneven hillside, cutting a path through the trees. It was quite a climb for a guy whose extent of daily physical activity consists of running up and down a flight of stairs. As I chose my way down the slope I spied the tops of pitched tents and the topaz gleam of Lake Senex. On the edge of the camp I could see a couple of Land Rovers and a green pickup truck. A number of people moved between the tents. No one seemed concerned with concealment.

A branch cracked behind me and I turned.

"Stop right there!" a female voice commanded.

Halting mid-turn, I slid a few inches in the pine needles and loose soil.

"*Hold it!*" she shrilled.

I had an impression of dark hair, spectacles and a purple Icelandic sweater. She was a small girl but she was holding a big gun.

I said politely, "I'm trying."

"Put your hands up."

I put my hands up, slid again and grabbed for the low hanging branch of a pine tree.

There was a loud explosion and something tore through the branches over my head, sending splinters and bits of pine everywhere.

"Whoops!" squealed the girl.

"Jesus!" I yelled, cowering behind the all-too-skinny tree trunk. "Are you crazy?"

"It just went off."

From the camp below us resounded sounds of alarm, and several flannel-shirted people swarmed up the hillside towards us, voices echoing in the hollow hills.

"Amy? Amy? Where are you?" Their voices drifted up to us.

"Here!" cried Amy. The gun wavered wildly.

We were reached first by a tall, gaunt middle-aged man wearing glasses, and a young, capable-looking guy in jeans and a camouflage vest.

The young guy grabbed and planted me face down in the dried pine needles with a speed and efficiency that left me speechless.

"Okay, Amy?" he demanded over my belated objections.

The older man was questioning, "What happened?" Trying to

make himself heard over the general confusion.

"I found him trespassing," Amy informed them excitedly. "The gun just went off."

"*Gun?* What gun?" exclaimed the older man. The owner of the knee in my spine echoed that dismay. He relaxed his armlock for a moment.

I rolled over and sat up, spitting out moldering tree bark and swear words.

"Trespassing? This is my property. Who the hell *are* you maniacs?"

The older man made ineffectual shushing motions. Amy pointed the gun at me again; it was snatched from her by the younger man who vaguely reminded me of Riordan with his blonde, built-for-action look.

"Hey!" protested Amy.

"Hey yourself," he shot back. "You know you're not supposed to be packing."

'Be packing?' Is this the way college kids talk nowadays? Are weapons that common on campus?

Oh yeah, I had them pegged for academics despite the hardware; the possible exception was the young tough who had manhandled me so efficiently.

His eyes met mine. They were green and apologetic. I don't subscribe to the gaydar theory but as our gazes locked, a flash of recognition went through me like a light turning on.

The older man was asking who I was as we were joined by two more field trip escapees: a middle-aged woman wearing a red bandana, and a handsome silver-haired man who appeared to have just set off on safari.

"My name is English," I bit out. "I own this land. Who are you?"

"Dr Philip Marquez. This is Amy –"

"Dr Lawrence Shoup," the chap in the safari hat interrupted in one of those imperious English accents.

Neither of us offered to shake hands as we looked each other up and down; granted he had the advantage since I was still on my ass.

When the Snub Direct had reached a stalemate, the woman in the bandana said, "But if you're Mr English, you gave us permission to dig here."

"I gave you permission to dig? Dig what? Who *are* you people?" I made to stand and the blond guy gave me a hand up. We hurriedly disengaged.

"Dr Philip Marquez," Marquez began again patiently. He was stopped cold by Stewart Granger.

"I am in charge of this expedition," Dr Shoup announced, "in the absence of Dr Livingston. Dr Livingston, the site supervisor, is the one who wrote you."

"Wrote *me*? Wrote me about what?" I paused in brushing down my clothes. Pine needles in my boots. Pine sap in my hair. I hated these people, whoever they were.

Dr Shoup frowned. "Regarding the excavation. The *site*. We are attempting to reconstruct the original site of the Red Rover mining camp."

At my incredulous look he said testily, "Perhaps you've forgotten? I assure you the proper forms have been filled out and documented with the Department of Parks and Recreation."

"This is private property, not state land."

"Well... that is, well..." I could see he wasn't used to being contradicted.

"Can I see these consent forms or whatever they are?"

"They are at the University."

"What University?"

"He means the local JC," the blond said dryly. "Tuolumne College."

"Yes, quite right," Shoup said as though this were a point for his side.

"They might be in Dr Livingston's papers," put in Amy, teacher's trigger happy pet.

"Dr Livingston took his briefcase with him," the middle-aged woman said.

"Not all his papers were in the briefcase, Bernice."

"Let's discuss this at base camp, shall we?" Dr Shoup suggested.

At base camp I was issued a folding stool, a cup of chicory coffee and an explanation of sorts from Kevin, the blond grad student, while Bernice, Marquez and Amy searched the site supervisor's papers for proof that I had granted permission to dig the test pits now pockmarking the face of the hillside.

"I guess we're all a little jumpy," Kevin apologised. "Some weird things have happened lately."

"You're telling me."

"Let's not bore Mr English with our problems, O'Reilly," Dr Shoup put in.

Naturally this made me curious. "What kinds of weird things have happened?"

Kevin and Dr Shoup exchanged one of those sliding glances people share when they aren't sure their stories will match.

Kevin said, "Noises and stuff."

"Coyotes," Dr Shoup said.

The things coyotes took the rap for in these parts was quite extraordinary.

"Practical jokes in all probability," Dr Shoup added.

"My dog was killed," Kevin said.

"That was certainly coyotes, O'Reilly."

Kevin looked unconvinced.

"What kind of dog?" I asked. Not that it was pertinent; I just wondered.

"Border collie. He was young and healthy and he'd been in fights before. I've never seen coyotes do that to a dog."

"Do what?"

"Tore him to pieces."

Shoup made an impatient movement. Kevin said, "Okay, what about the chanting?"

"Chanting?"

"Local yokels," opined Dr Shoup. I figured with that attitude, he must be a real hit here in Hicksville.

About this time, Dr Marquez and his cohorts returned triumphantly waving a sheet of paper.

"I knew I'd seen it," Bernice announced.

Taking the letter, I studied it. There, on a Xeroxed copy of my letterhead, someone had typed to the effect that, for the sum of $50.00 a week, the Archeology Department of Tuolumne Junior College had permission to dig for the Red Rover mining camp. There were no conditions and no restrictions.

"I never wrote this. That's not my signature." It was not my signature but it looked like a rough tracing of it. I scrutinized the date.

"This is p-preposterous," Dr Shoup stuttered into the silence that followed my words.

"I agree."

"It's got your name on it," Amy informed me.

"I see that."

"This doesn't make sense," Dr Marquez said, slowly scratching what appeared to be an impressive hickey on his throat.

"Lawrence?"

"Lawrence" appeared to be Dr Shoup who lost no time launching his offensive. "What exactly are you trying to pull here, young man?" He said to me.

"What is your precious Dr Livingston trying to pull?" I retorted nastily. I'd had a bitch of a day, and getting shot at and thrown down a hillside had not improved my mindset. There were horrified gasps from the womenfolk as though I'd accused Louis Leakey of salting the fossil beds.

"Do you realise what you're suggesting, sir?"

"There's probably a simple explanation," Kevin interjected.

"Sure. It's a forgery."

They stared at me – or glared, as dispositions warranted – and I could see it cross a couple of minds that they should have let Amy shoot me back there in the trees.

Which reminded me of the man who had been shot. Suppose Annie Oakley had got carried away on guard duty and the others were covering for her?

Okay, a little thin, but I *had* seen a dead man in the middle of my dirt road and he had disappeared without a trace an hour later. Who shot him? Why? And what had become of his body? These folks were my nearest neighbors.

I said, "I never received this letter. I sure as hell never wrote this reply. Look, they've misspelled 'gratuity.'" As though this were conclusive proof.

"Who did?" Kevin O'Reilly looked sheepish as soon as the words left his mouth.

"It looks to me like someone took a copy of a letter I sent them, typed their own message in the blanked out body, and then traced my signature."

"Who?" asked Amy and Bernice, still kind of missing the point.

"Why?" Marquez and Kevin chorused at the same time.

"I don't know. Someone who wanted fifty bucks a week." I thought I had a pretty good idea actually, since I recalled mailing a check in February to my legendary caretaker, Ted Harvey.

"I suppose you're going to try and renege on your agreement," Dr Shoup said.

"I'm not reneging on anything. I don't know that I want you digging holes in the scenery until I hear more about your little venture."

"'Little venture?'" The woman in the red bandana repeated indignantly. How to win friends and influence people, that was me.

"When Dr Livingston returns he will straighten this out," Amy huffed. Marquez and Shoup looked less certain.

"I shall contact the University's legal department," Dr Shoup informed me grandly.

I thought of dear old Mr Gracen, our family solicitor, who had spent the last sixty years writing and rewriting wills for clients even more aged and infirm than himself. I tried to picture him going toe to toe with lawyers who actually litigated for a living. I hoped the stress wouldn't finish him. I said, "Fine. Maybe you can get together your paperwork so I can get an idea of what you're trying to do here."

'Accomplish' might have been a more tactful word, I realised, as they bristled and muttered amongst themselves.

Our meeting ended. In distrust and suspicion they watched me hike up the hill escorted by Kevin O'Reilly who appeared uncomfortable in the role of bouncer.

At the crest of the hill Kevin said, "Uh... sorry about this."

"Me too." Somehow I never pictured myself standing in the way of higher education. "It could still work out, but I need a clearer

picture of your operation. I've never heard of the Red Rover mine."
It would have made more sense if they were exploring the Indian
caves (not that I would have agreed to that either).

"I guess Dr Shoup rubbed you the wrong way. He rubs everyone
the wrong way, but he's the real thing."

"You don't have to tell me." A card-carrying prick if I ever
met one.

"I mean, he's got the credentials. He trained at Oxford. He
worked at the British Museum. He's a member of every society you
can name: The Society of Historical Archeology, The National
Science Foundation. He writes for *National Geographic*."

Uh huh.

"Anyway, Livingston's in charge here. He's cool. You'll see."

The boyish enthusiasm was kind of cute. "Sure."

Kevin hesitated. "So – last night that was probably you blasting
Con Te Partiro?"

The hills are alive with the sound of Muzak.

"I thought I was alone out here."

He was smiling at me in a steady appreciative way and I quipped
idiotically, "My mating call."

"Yeah?"

"No."

We both laughed and I trudged down my side of the mountain.

The rest of the day passed uneventfully. After lunch I got ambitious and hunted down the goose-feather mattresses which had
been wrapped in plastic and stored in the attic. After a wrestling
match during which the mattress nearly threw me down the narrow stairs, I dragged its lumpy carcass into the bedroom I had used
when I was a kid. This groundfloor room had a great view of the
distant snowy mountains. I made up the four poster bed and spent

the next couple of hours clearing bird nests out the chimney flue. I'm a creature who likes his comforts.

My own nesting instinct satisfied, I settled down with a stack of books and read for several hours. Busily checking copyright dates and printings as booksellers will, I made the discovery that Leslie Ford had developed a second, masculine pseudonym. Under the nom de plume, 'David Frome' she wrote a dozen mysteries featuring a frail male sleuth named Mr Pinkerton who, with the help of a stalwart Scotland Yard inspector, solved a variety of homicides. Comparisons were inevitable and depressing.

Fed up with Leslie and myself I tossed aside *Mr Pinkerton Finds a Body* and warmed up the laptop.

Several pages of data entry later, I concluded that the change of scenery had not improved my masterpiece. I was beginning to wonder if anything could.

The foil rolled drunkenly across the floor, the hilt nudging Jason's toe.
"Pick it up," ordered Lucius.
"Pick it up yourself."

"Jeez, Jason. You can do better than that," I muttered.

"Are you sure you want to do this?" I typed.

Was I? Definitely not. Maybe a quote from the bard? I reached for my copy of *Titus*.

?!

My copy of *Titus* was still in LA. I dealt with that for a moment, decided it probably wasn't *really* the last straw, and resumed wordsmithing.

On I slogged till about ten-thirty, developing carpal tunnel syndrome if nothing else.

Stopping for a breather, I ended up in the kitchen. I was pouring myself a glass of Merlot from one of the local wineries when I noticed the light was back on in Ted Harvey's trailer.

Had the prodigal returned? I grabbed my jacket and trucked on out to the trailer. I was halfway across the yard when the light went out. I peered at my watch in the moonlight: 11:45.

Late for a social call, but I was way past the social niceties.

Reaching the trailer, I hammered on the door.

Nothing happened.

I pounded again and then I tried the handle. The door opened, hinges protesting loudly.

Dimly, I had an impression of movement above me and then an explosion of pain blew through my head.

That was the last thing I remember.

Four

When I opened my eyes, I was in a narrow hospital bed with railings. There were electrodes taped to my chest and an IV stuck in my arm. Not a good start to any day (or night, judging by the muted lights around me). Waking in hospitals is #1 on my Secret Dread list, but before I could really work myself into a sweat, the thumping started on the ceiling of my brain. I played dead, hoping the pain would forget me and lumber on its way.

"What the hell happened?"

I thought I was complaining to myself, but I must have mumbled it aloud because a familiar voice to my left said, "I guess that's more original than 'where am I.'"

Very very carefully I turned my head. The green line on the heart monitor jumped nervously as I met the lynx-eyed gaze of LAPD Detective Jake Riordan.

"What are you doing here?" I guess I sounded more querulous than flattered. I suspected he was a hallucination; he sure wasn't a result of the pain medication because I wasn't getting enough to smother the kettle drum thudding behind my eyes.

"The cops were curious about why you had a homicide detective's card in your wallet. They gave me a call."

"Oh." Did that answer my question?

He has nice eyes, does Riordan. Hazel in colour with long dark lashes; almost pretty, though there is nothing pretty about six foot plus of USDA prime. He studied me out of his nice hazel eyes and his mouth gave a kind of reluctant twitch. He shook his head, apparently over my sorry state.

"Who clocked me?"

"No idea. You called it in yourself."

"I what?"

"You picked your concussed ass up, walked inside and phoned 911 before you passed out again."

"No way. I'd remember that."

"You were on automatic pilot maybe."

"I couldn't have." I didn't feel like I could manage it now, let alone minutes after I'd been coshed.

"Baby, I heard the tape. It was you."

I thought this over wearily. "How would you hear the tape?"

"The sheriffs had me listen to it thinking maybe your assailant phoned for help."

This sounded confusing as hell.

Riordan stood up, checked the IV drip beside the bed. "Shit. You're running on empty." He went to the door and said something to someone outside.

A matronly lady in a mint-coloured smock bustled in, clucked over my fallen form and went out. Jake looked pissed, which I didn't have the energy to deal with.

I closed my eyes.

"There *is* life after death," Jake remarked the next time I surfaced.

"Hey."

"Hey yourself." His eyes were red, like he'd spent a sleepless night. He was leaning over the bed rail, and I had the strangest impression that he had been holding my hand – which tells you how doped I was.

"What were we talking about?"

"When?"

"Before."

"We were discussing how you managed to get knocked cold by someone searching Ted Harvey's trailer."

"How do you know someone was searching the trailer?"

"Baby, you explained it all when you made your famous 911 call." He looked like he was trying not to snicker at some memory.

"Famous?"

Jake nodded. "They were discussing it over at Granny Parker's Pantry when I had breakfast this morning."

Breakfast? What time was it now?

"How long have I been here? Where *am* I exactly?"

"Almost forty-eight hours. You are in Calavares County Hospital running up a sizable bill even as we speak. I hope you've got health insurance."

I hoped I had enough. I've known solvent, gainfully-employed people bankrupted by a hospital stay.

"Next question: when can I leave?"

Jake looked vague. "A day or two. They want to keep an eye on you."

I knew what that meant.

"They've had a plenty good look already." I hate hospitals. When I die I don't want it to be in some hospital. I started feeling around the IV needle, raised my head and checked out the technology on my bare chest. Instant Panic: just add water. "I want to talk to the doctor. I want to go home."

Jake planted his hand on my shoulder. It was like having a brick dropped on my chest. "Simmer down, baby." He traced my collarbone with his thumb. I couldn't have moved if I had wanted to; I was too surprised to try. "Just relax."

The feel of his callused thumb on my sensitized skin was weirdly hypnotic. I blinked up at him like I had been shot by a tranquilizer dart.

"When they brought you in, your heartbeat was a little funky. It's been fine for twenty-four hours so they're going to release you pretty soon. Okay?"

I assented weakly.

Jake made a fist and hooked a playful right to the angle of my jaw.

"Did they find Harvey?" I asked a while later, a coherent thought bubbling up from the bog of physical misery.

Jake paused from squeezing drops in his eyes. "No. No sign of Harvey. Is he the one who crowned you?"

"I didn't see who hit me. I opened the door to the trailer. That's the last thing I remember."

"Why did you go out there?"

"I saw a light on. I thought maybe he was back." I tried to remember. It seemed like a long time ago. "The night before, someone was prowling around outside the house."

"Searching for something?"

"I guess. But what?"

"Harvey?"

"Unless Harvey is the prowler."

Jake considered this from a cop's perspective. "Then who was your DB in the road Thursday night?"

"You believe me?"

"Yeah, I believe you. Why did you hang up like that on Saturday? And why the hell didn't you tell that ghoul who works for you where you'd gone?"

This brought back a number of things I had conveniently forgotten, like the chick he was in bed with when I called. I said stiffly, "I got the impression you didn't... take me seriously."

A couple of beats counted out by the heart monitor. Jake wore an odd expression.

"I take you seriously."

Were we talking bodies in the road or in the bed?

A nurse entered from the wings and did the usual stage business with thermometer, blood pressure cuff and clipboard. I tried to remain stoic under her icy hands.

"You're obviously feeling better," she said cheerfully. She appeared to be talking to Jake, who gave her a boyish grin.

"Those antihistamines worked like magic."

The nurse dimpled.

I said irritably, "When can I go home?"

"Oh, that's up to Doctor."

No definite article. 'Doctor,' like in 'God.'

"When does he show up?"

"He'll be making his rounds this afternoon." Right after the burning bush shtick.

"Could you let him know I plan on checking out today? Like now."

She tittered at this witticism and departed stage right on a breeze of antiseptic.

The doctor hemmed and hawed and advised against discharging myself before he sounded the all clear. Jake folded his arms across his brawny chest, watching with interest as me and the doc duked it out. The doc had medicine, experience and logic on his side. He was no match for me. Shaky but stubborn, I sat there in my chic backless gown peeling off the lime-green plastic hospital bracelet, demanding an 'Against Medical Advice'.

"We can't hold you prisoner," the man of medicine admitted when pressed.

I delivered the *coup de grâce*. "My insurance won't cover another day."

Open sesame. Two hours later I watched Jake scowl as his Acura singled its city-bred way down the unforgiving dirt road that led to the Pine Shadow. We had stopped in town just long enough for Jake to pick his gear up from the Twain Harte Inn. He had traveled light, seemingly planning on nothing more than a stopover.

"Right up ahead is where I found him," I said as we bounced over the cattle guard.

"Here?" Jake rolled to a stop.

Like yellow mist, mustard flower seemed to float across the valley, drifting over the green hillsides in the afternoon breeze.

I opened my door and Jake said, "Stay put, Adrien. I know how to investigate a crime scene."

I subsided, watching through the windshield as Jake tiptoed through the tules. He walked out several yards and circled back. At the side of the road he knelt down and examined the brush.

Jake sneezed mightily, blowing petals from the surrounding wildflowers and stomped back to the car.

"Well?"

He shrugged, mopping his nose with a flag-sized hanky. "Too much time has passed. The underbrush over there has been knocked down; possibly a car or a truck pulling around. That doesn't mean it was used to cart off your DB." He released the brake.

I said, "Jake, there's something else. I've got a team of amateur archeologists from the local JC camped out on the back of my property. They've got a forged letter giving them permission to dig for a lost mining camp."

"What do you mean, 'forged'?"

I didn't have a chance to answer, because as we drove into the front yard I spotted the sheriff's black and white pickup. The sheriff himself stood on my front porch flanked by his faithful deputy.

"What the hell now?" Jake growled.

We braked and got out. The sheriff marched down the wooden steps.

"English, you're under arrest," he announced.

"Say what?"

"You heard."

My heart began to pound with adrenaline in the Fight or Flight response. Since my normal reflex is flight, I'm not sure why I reacted with a surge of scared aggression, but I did. My fists balled up and I launched forward, only to find my way blocked by Jake.

"Whoa," he said. He turned to Billingsly, asking, "What's the charge, Sheriff?"

Billingsly said flatly, "English has about an acre of pot growing on the hill behind this house. How about a charge of manufacturing marijuana with intent to distribute?"

"I've been here four days," I said. "How am I supposed to have achieved these results? Miracle-Gro?"

"It's your property, it's your pot," Billingsly said without emotion. "But if you don't think the charge fits, try this for size: aiding and abetting, or conspiring, in the possession and production of a controlled substance – with intent to distribute."

So... reducing the charges to 'constructive possession,' what was that? Five years minimum? It was so unreal, for a moment I felt like I was on drugs.

The deputy actually had the handcuffs out.

My voice rose in tempo to the blood beating in my temples. "Obviously you should be looking for Ted Harvey, the guy I apparently pay to sit in the sun and smoke dope all day. Obviously –" My heart was stuttering in fear and anger. Jake put his hand on my arm in warning – which did not go unnoticed.

Jake said, "Can I ask you boys how you came to be searching the hill behind Mr English's house?"

"We've got a warrant," Dwayne chimed in.

Billingsly looked annoyed at unauthorised vocalization. "We got an anonymous tip," he said.

"And that doesn't seem suspicious to you?" I cried.

"Listen, English, the pot is *there*. And I notice you didn't seem surprised to hear it."

"I notice you seem more interested in anonymous phone calls than the fact I nearly got brained on my own property. Why's that? One anonymous phone call and you're out here like a flash, but an honest taxpayer is in the hospital two days and you never even show up to take his statement?"

Yep, I was losing it. Jake must have deduced it was time to intervene. He said mildly enough, "I don't know how you boys handle things up here, but I'd say this is a lawsuit waiting to happen. English is barely out of the hospital."

"They released him. If he's well enough to leave the hospital –"

Dwayne jumped in. "Maybe you LA cops turn a blind eye to smokin' dope and –"

"AND YOU'VE GOT A FART'S CHANCE IN A HURRICANE OF BRINGING THIS TO TRIAL," Jake overrode them both loudly.

There was a pause in the wake of that lung power. The windmill screeched rustily in the breeze. Pretty much expressing my feelings.

"Before your DA laughs you out of his office you might want to consider the lawsuit English will slap on you," Jake added coolly. "That's you *personally*, you follow me? You'll have liens on your wages; your home and your car, if not your wife and kids. Think about it. Long after Mr English has gone back to Los Angeles, you'll still be negotiating with his lawyers."

I can't say I appreciated this line of defense and the portrait of me as a litigation-crazed Angeleno, but it was effective – as I could see by the way Deputy Dwayne sort of sidled away from his boss's side. Billingsly's piggy eyes flickered as he mentally squared-off against my high-priced, big city lawyers, a long distance nemesis he would have no power to touch.

A gigantic tumbleweed rolled by while we waited for the sheriff to make up his mind.

Billingsly stroked his finger down the white skunk stripe in his beard.

I reassured myself that if they did arrest me, Jake would handle it. He would know what to do. He would have me out on bail in hours. No need to panic. I told myself this two or three times while the back of my shirt grew damp with perspiration.

"Let me give you a friendly piece of advice, *boys*," Billingsly managed finally. "You rile the wrong people, and you'll be too busy planning your funerals to worry about going to court."

"Never use the word 'obvious' to a hick cop," Jake said as we watched the two-man posse ride away in a cloud of exhaust and dust. "Let alone three times in one breath."

"Thanks for the tip. Any secret handshakes you can show me?" I turned towards the house. I needed to sit before I caved in; the roof of my skull felt like it was cracking apart, showering my brain with dust and pebbles. "So how long are you staying?" I asked politely, trying to unlock the front door. My hands were shaking. Jake took the keys and let us inside.

"Just until you're fit to drive back to LA."

"I'm staying."

"What do you mean, you're staying? You live in Los Angeles, remember?"

"I'm staying till I find out what the *fuck* is going on here!"

Jake said nothing.

I knew what he was thinking. "If I leave this place now there's going to be a midnight barbecue to guarantee I never have reason to come back."

"You stick around and you may wake up in the middle of a midnight barbecue."

"I'll take my chances."

Jake snorted. "Tough guy, huh?"

"Yeah, that's me."

"Reality check, tough guy. You've got a faulty pump, savvy? That automatically disqualifies you from the Hardy Boys club."

Now why this simple statement of fact pissed me off so much, I'm not sure. Especially since it was what I'd been telling myself for days.

"Nobody's asking you to stay." More effective I guess if my voice hadn't gone high and quavery with stress.

"I noticed."

"Nobody asked you to ride to my rescue. You want to bail, don't let me stop you."

Jake's lips quirked as though he actually found this funny. "This is the thanks the cavalry gets?"

"You want a big, wet, sloppy kiss hello?" I slapped my forehead. "I forgot. You don't do that."

Silence.

"Okaaaay," Jake said finally. "You want to say what's on your mind?"

"I've said it," I said crankily.

Silence.

"I'm going to lie down. You know, get some shut-eye before the barbecue starts. Check and see if we have marshmallows, will you?"

I threw myself on the sofa too fagged for the moment to care what anybody, including Jake, did. The sofa made a couple of slow wide swoops, like a merry-go-round drawing to a standstill. I closed my eyes.

I could sense Jake standing there in the middle of the room, a perplexed Colossus of Rhodes. That's right, big boy, I thought. Do the math.

I was drifting out on the tide of peaceful oblivion when he muttered, "Now who the hell is *this?*"

Five

I sat up. Jake looked as irritated as if the baby had been woken from its nap.

"Who is it?" I questioned.

Jake shrugged. "Some kid in a green pickup."

I went out on to the front porch flanked by Jake. Kevin O'Reilly, Boy Archeologist, was climbing out of one of those battered green forester trucks (minus the ranger insignia).

"Howdy," he called.

Boy Howdy, in fact.

"Hey."

"I heard you had an accident. I came over to see how you're doing."

"A-okay."

A little self-consciously he handed over a two-pound box of See's candy. "I don't know if you like chocolate."

"Who doesn't like chocolate?"

"I don't like chocolate," said Jake right behind me.

Kevin looked Jake up and down. Jake looked Kevin up and down.

"This is my friend, Jake Riordan," I introduced Kevin. "Kevin's one of the archeologists I was telling you about."

"Kevin O'Reilly," Kevin said offering a hand.

They shook; I was relieved it didn't turn into an arm wrestling match then and there. It was funny because Kevin did look like a younger version of Jake. They could have been cousins. Same gene pool.

"A pleasure to meet you – sir," Kevin added blandly. Jake's eyes narrowed as though he were amused. I think it was amusement.

"Uh huh. You're camped where exactly, Kevin?"

Kevin pointed out the ridge. "We're right back behind that little mountain. In Spaniard's Hollow."

"Walking distance?"

"Sure."

"Come in and have a cup of coffee," I invited.

"No, I've got to get back." Kevin glanced at Jake standing there like a monolith at my shoulder. "Dr Shoup wanted to invite you to have dinner with us. We can show you around the site, answer any questions. Maybe reach an agreement before the lawyers get involved."

"Sure. When?"

"Tonight."

God not tonight, I moaned inwardly in an unsleuth-like spirit that would have bitterly disappointed Grace Latham. So it was actually a relief when Jake ground out, "We've got plans."

"Tomorrow night?"

"Yes," I said with a glance at Jake.

"Great," Kevin said. He smiled at me, his green eyes warm. "Glad to see you're up and around, Adrien."

"Thanks."

Jake and I walked back inside as Kevin reversed in a wide arc and drove away.

"That was nice of him," I said.

"Uh huh."

"The others are more Poindexter. You'll see. If you stick around, that is."

"Yeah?" Jake didn't sound particularly interested. "What's the fishing like around here?" He shut the door with a small bang that sent my nerves jumping.

"Fishing or trolling?"

"Fishing."

"Good, I think. I don't know about Lake Senex, but the rivers are full of trout and bass." We were talking about fishing?

"I should have brought my poles. I guess I can rent a couple in town when I pick up a fishing licence."

"Planning on staying?"

"Just till you wise up."

"I'm flattered you think that's a possibility."

"Yeah, well it's lucky I have a lot of back vacation."

I tottered back to the couch and Jake asked, "You want some lunch?"

"Bastard." I added fretfully, "Can't you hear the tom-toms?"

"No. What do they say?"

"White man need more pain killer."

"I thought you were the strong silent type."

"*Me?* You're obviously thinking of one of your leatherboy friends."

I kept my eyes closed during the charged pause that followed this. At last Jake said mildly, "Since you're feeling chatty, maybe you'll fill me in on the drug charges."

I rubbed my temples and said, "It's a frame. My belief is Ted Harvey planted that crop."

"Ted Harvey being your handyman?"

"Not so handy as it turns out."

"What's your arrangement with him?"

"He lives here rent free. I pay the utilities and a hundred bucks a month for him to keep an eye on the place. He's supposed to take care of any repairs, and arrange to have someone from town come and clean up every so often."

"Aren't you the guy always short of cash?"

"Yes, and if I had any brains I'd sell the place." But it had been in my family for over a century. Nor would I ever be able to afford anything comparable on my own.

"And your theory is that Harvey is growing and selling pot on the back of your property?"

"I don't know about selling it, although he seems like an enterprising chap; I think he forged a letter to the Tuolumne College Archeology Department."

"Why?"

"Why did he forge it?"

Patiently Jake reined me in. "Why do you think Harvey forged it?"

"For one thing, he's the only person in a four hundred mile radius who had access to my stationary or signature. For another, the college was instructed to make checks payable to the Pine Shadow Ranch."

"To the ranch?"

"As though it were a business entity, you see? Then Harvey, I'll make you a bet, cashed those checks locally without any hitch, because everyone knows he handles the ranch maintenance."

"But you don't know this for a fact?"

"I didn't have a chance to check on it."

"It's not bad," Jake admitted. "Small towns tend to be informal about that kind of thing. Everybody knows Harvey, knows he works for you. Someone might assume you had authorised him to act on your behalf; that would set a precedent."

"A little forgery, a little larceny, a little chicanery. I wonder which one got him killed – and why the body was moved."

"Now that's a jump."

"When I described the man I'd seen to the sheriff, the first name he suggested was Ted Harvey."

"But he'd think of Harvey anyway since Harvey lives on the premises."

That was true. I hadn't considered that.

"But Harvey's missing."

"Says who? How do you know he's not on a fishing trip?"

"His truck is here."

"Maybe he's with friends. Or he could be laying low. How do you know *he* didn't hit you?"

"Why would he?"

"Maybe he doesn't like visitors after ten o'clock? Maybe he's used to dealing with folks less civilised than yourself?" He headed for the kitchen. "What do you have to eat around here?"

I left him to figure it out, leaning back and closing my eyes. Jake had a point. I needed to see a recent picture of Harvey. Criminal investigation begins with the victim. At this point we were not for sure who our victim was.

After a few minutes of trying to convince myself I didn't feel so bad it struck me that I had really underplayed this concussion thing in my own writing. Jason Leland was routinely knocked on his noggin and an hour later was back to chasing bad guys backstage, upstage and all around the town. The reality was a shattering headache to end all headaches, a touch of nausea and pulverised neck and shoulder muscles. But at least the old ticker was still keeping time.

*

When I woke up, Jake was outside reducing the timberline to a pile of kindling. For a time I stood at the window admiring the bronzed musculature of his bare chest as he sweated and chopped wood with manly ferocity. He looked at home out here on the range, his blond hair shining like miner's gold in the mountain breeze.

A beautiful man, I thought with an inward sigh.

I wandered into the kitchen and found canned stew simmering on the back burner. A taste off the wooden spoon informed me Jake had doctored it up with several cloves of garlic and the vintage Tabasco sauce in the cupboard. If anything could clear his sinuses it was this recipe.

I was having a bowl when Jake walked in buttoning up his shirt.

"You look better," he observed giving me a close look.

"I feel better."

Jake went over to the stove and dished out a bowl of stew. Getting a beer out of the fridge, he sat down across from me.

"You know we could probably pay someone to drive the Bronco. You could come back to LA with me."

"I already told you –"

"I know what you said, now hear me out."

I waited.

"I think maybe you have stumbled on to something here. I checked out Harvey's trailer while you were sleeping and I'm pretty sure it's been ransacked."

"I think it always looks like that."

"Drawers emptied out, the couch cushions and bed mattress ripped open? The fridge dumped over?"

"Well, no."

Jake studied me thoughtfully. "If Harvey's dealing then you may have wandered into the middle of a local drug war."

"*Here?* In Calavares County?"

"You scare me when you say things like that," Jake said seriously.

I guess it did sound a little *Our Town*ish. "Okay, I know the drug problem has reached the suburbs, but this doesn't *feel* like a drug deal gone bad."

"Please don't use the word intuition to me or I will slug you. Aren't you the guy who told me one of the golden rules is that detectives may not solve the crime by use of intuition and/or acts of God?"

Jeez, who knew he was listening that closely? "That's in books, Jake," I protested. "Aren't you the guy who told me a cop's gut instinct is one of his best tools?"

"You're not a cop, baby. You're a bookseller. You don't have a gut instinct. You have a knack for nearly getting yourself killed."

I batted my lashes. "I didn't know you cared."

"The hell you didn't."

"What can happen with you here to protect me?"

Jake made a sound somewhere between a snort and a laugh which blew soup from his spoon across the table. How could you resist such a big lug?

"Just don't say I didn't warn you," he said.

After dinner, Jake built up a bonfire in the fireplace and we had coffee and See's candy for dessert. For a guy who didn't like chocolate, Jake consumed his fair share. He also showed a propensity to lick his fingers. I found this distracting; the slide of his pink tongue up his naked finger. He had big hands, strong hands, but the fingers were long and sensitive, and I kept wondering what those hands would feel like on my body.

"Here's mud in your eye," I said, and Jake and I clinked coffee mugs. I'm not sure what was in his but mine was straight coffee.

Concussion and alcohol don't mix, although by now my headache merely felt like the worst hangover of my life.

Despite his misgivings, Jake seemed more relaxed than I'd ever seen him. I speculated it was because we were so thoroughly alone, unobserved by curious or judging eyes.

"How's the book going?" he asked idly, glancing at my open laptop. "What's it called, *Death for a Ducat?*"

"Wrong play. You're thinking of *Hamlet.*" Jake snorted at the idea he would be thinking of any such thing. "Mine's based on *Titus Andronicus*, the play so bad Shakespearean scholars have tried for centuries to prove Shakespeare didn't write it."

"Good choice. So tell me what your book's about."

Actually I had told him several times what my book was about, but I had known then he wasn't really listening. I offered the highlights and Jake rolled his eyes or shook his head depending on how far out of touch with reality my plot machinations seemed.

"Aren't you supposed to write what you know?"

"What do I know? I'm a thirty-something gay man with a weak heart. I sell books for a living. Who wants to read about that?"

"Good point."

"I don't have a lot of practical experience with crime."

"You seem to be a magnet for it though."

"Don't try to cheer me up."

Jake grinned his crooked grin and reached for another chocolate. "It is a little suspicious from a cop's perspective."

I set my coffee cup on the wooden floor and stretched widely. Despite the coffee I was crashing.

"How old is this place?" Jake queried, staring up at the blackened ceiling beams.

I focused on him with an effort. "This room was part of the original stage stop. It was built in 1847. The rest of the building isn't quite as old. My great great-grandfather started ranching in the early 1900s. He added on to the existing structure."

"It's a nice chunk of property."

I nodded.

Jake seemed to be pursuing a train of thought. He eyed the stacks of books which I had neatly separated into paperbacks and hardcovers. "So this is kind of a working vacation for you?"

I guessed that he was sort-of probing what had triggered my Bat-Outta-Hell. *Speak now or forever hold your peace*, I warned myself.

"Yeah, something like that. Turns out Granna was a mystery buff. She's got a collection here of first editions to rival the Library of Congress." I filled him in on the thrilling discovery that my favourite mystery writer had a male pseudonym. "I've got this theory that Inspector Bull and Mr Pinkerton are closeted gays."

I was mostly joking but Jake said crisply, "See, that's the kind of queer thinking I despise. According to the fags, everybody who's anybody was really homosexual. You name it. Michelangelo, Alexander Hamilton, Errol Flynn, Walt Whitman. It's pathetic."

His angry scorn silenced me.

"You're just kidding yourself if you believe being a fag is common or normal or some lifestyle choice."

"I don't think it's a choice. It isn't for me anyway."

He said bitterly, "It sure as hell isn't for me."

If it were, Jake would choose not to be gay. No news there. I rubbed my forehead trying to smooth away the pain there. Jake continued to glower into the fireplace, the shadows flickering across his profile.

Cowboy wisdom: never itch for something you ain't willing to scratch for.

"I'm going to turn in," I said.

No answer.

I rose and went into the bedroom, stripped off and rolled myself in my sleeping bag, the flannel feeling like a caress on my aching body. I sighed and then nearly jumped out of my skin when Jake spoke from right above me.

"Roll over. I'll rub your back for you."

"Uh –" My voice made a sound it hadn't made since it changed.

I turned on my belly and Jake unzipped my bag like you'd unpeel something soft and vulnerable in its shell, which is how I felt as he laid his big hands on my shoulders.

"Relax."

Oh sure. I caught my breath then expelled it as Jake rested his palm on the small of my back. He didn't move, didn't speak. I waited until I seemed to feel the heat of his fingers spreading out through my nerves and muscles all the way to my genitals. He pressed down gently and I could feel my spine lengthening, my hips spreading. He stayed like that for about a minute and I was very relaxed indeed, my body basking in that healing warmth.

Jake placed his other palm in front of his hand and slowly, deliberately pushed it up the length of my spine as though smoothing away the kinks, vertebra by vertebra, until the pads of his fingers pressed into the base of my skull. He gave the back of my neck a gentle squeeze and I shivered with pleasure.

Jake repeated this sliding motion over and over until I was melting through the flannel bag lining into the ticking of the old mattress. I felt flushed, boneless, utterly at ease. My head stopped hurting for the first time since I'd left the hospital. You hear about the healing power of touch; I felt it now – a laying-on of hands.

At long last Jake's hands stilled.

"Good-night," he said quietly.

"'Night," I murmured, on the edge of sleep.

A moment later sleep disappeared in a jolt of awareness as Jake kissed the nape of my neck... and departed.

Six

Judging from the small off-colour mushroom cloud hanging over the hill the next morning, it appeared that Sheriff Billingsly and the county were waging war on drugs.

Jake suggested we drive into Basking for breakfast.

We wound up at Granny Parker's Pantry where we had the spacious dining room and a shady view of Main Street America all to ourselves.

We ordered from a large lady in a sunny yellow uniform that matched the building's exterior perfectly.

"After we eat I'm going to do some checking around," Jake remarked, tossing his menu aside. "Can you keep yourself entertained?"

"Am I supposed to shop while you sleuth?"

"I'm not sleuthing. I just want to check out a couple of things."

Into my silence he added, "One guy poking around asking questions is enough. Two is going to attract the wrong kind of attention."

The waitress brought our breakfast. Jake had his usual smorgasbord: slab of ham, four eggs, biscuits & gravy, and large orange juice. He regarded my bowl of oatmeal, forehead wrinkling.

"That's it? That's all you're eating?"

"Unlike you, I don't have to sustain the equivalent of a small country."

Unexpectedly, he reddened. "This is muscle, not fat."

I didn't doubt it. What I'd seen of Jake so far was all lean mean fighting machine. I was surprised he'd be sensitive about it.

"I didn't say you were fat. I said there was a lot of you."

With an evil glance, he subsided into his coffee cup. I realised the waitress had heard this exchange and was scandalised to the fibres of her hair net. Do heterosexual males not discuss weight? Was it something in the tone of our voices? Or was she alarmed because she had pegged us as the infamous dope dealing, 911-calling foreigners? Whatever it was, I hoped Jake didn't take notice. He was so comfortable under his imagined cloak of invisibility. I didn't want this vacation from his warped reality spoiled.

I had my third cup of coffee as Jake polished off the last of his fried eggs.

"I guess I could drop by the library. I need a copy of *Titus*. I forgot mine at home."

Jake nodded, not really listening.

"I've been thinking," he said at last, wiping his plate down with biscuit, "about who placed that anonymous phone call tipping off the sheriff to the pot."

"It could have been anyone. Hikers."

"Where are these archeologists camped? Just over that little mountain, aren't they?"

"Yes." I followed his line of reasoning. "Any one of them could have noticed the stuff growing and called the cops. But why?"

"Retaliation? You are threatening to pull the plug on their sandbox."

"Maybe." I dwelt on this. "That's pretty vindictive for a bunch of pottery-hunters." But were they all amateurs? Students were not technically amateurs. Dr Marquez and Dr Shoup were not students and did not strike me as amateurs either. Dr Shoup seemed like a man who took things – himself in particular – seriously. "Maybe there's another purpose behind calling the cops. Maybe they need me out of the way."

Jake looked pained. "'Out of the way?' Adrien –"

"No, listen a sec, Jake." Jake listened grimly. "Suppose the point of that phone call was to keep me busy with legal hassles so I wouldn't have time to worry abut who was digging what up where."

"Huh?"

"Suppose, just suppose, there's some – some – skulduggery going on in Spaniard's Hollow?"

"Don't tell me, let me guess," Jake said. "They're digging for buried treasure."

"Well, I don't know about that."

Jake's eyebrows rose. "You don't? That is something."

"It's just a theory."

"Or that crack on the head."

"Yes, and who hit me on the head, and why?"

"They weren't trying to kill you or they would have finished the job."

"Not kill me, just get me out of the way."

"Agreed," Jake said crisply, "because you got *in* the way of searching Harvey's trailer. That doesn't have anything to do with skulduggery in the mountains."

"It might."

"Last night you were talking about a cop's gut instinct. My gut instinct tells me these two things are not connected."

"Let's hope the equipment is functioning this time around," I said sweetly. "Two months ago your gut told you I was a psychopathic murderer."

Jake's eyes narrowed like a tiger who is tired of playing with his food.

"Hit rewind." He tapped his forehead with his index finger. "I didn't think you were a murderer. I thought you were not telling everything you knew, which was right. I thought you were not being stalked."

"Which was wrong."

"Which was..." He took a deep breath.

"Wrong," I prompted.

"Wrong," he conceded.

I grinned. "Just wanted to hear it."

Following breakfast we went our separate ways, agreeing to meet back at the car by noon.

I suspected the real reason Jake didn't want me playing Watson was he would be homing for the sheriff sub-station where I would be even more *persona non grata* than he. That was okay by me. I had my own hypothesis and I could do my own kind of footwork in the library.

I found the library wedged in between a coffeehouse and a feed store. It was the kind of place I love. The kind of place they don't build anymore. Weathered brick trimmed in white gingerbread; according to the brass placard by the front door, Basking Library had been built in 1923.

Inside, it was dark and quiet. Antique tables, lovingly polished over decades of scratches, gleamed in the light of green banker's lamps. Ceiling-high bookshelves were crammed with faded volumes. This was my turf just as the mean streets of LA were Jake's.

There was one computer, tied up by a pugnacious senior cross-referencing mysteries featuring feline detectives. Knowing that could take a while, I bee-lined for the librarian, requesting books on local history. She directed me toward Mark Twain and *Roughing It.*

"I was hoping for something on Basking itself. The gold rush years, mining history. Maybe lost mines?"

She looked stumped, but then brightened. "Our local historical society put together something like that a few years back. You can probably still buy a copy at Royale House. That's right around the corner."

"Marvellous."

From the way her eyes flickered behind the rhinestone-framed glasses, I gathered men in Basking did not go around chirping 'marvellous'. I gave her a reassuring smile and headed for the wooden card catalogue located beneath a display of artwork by patients of the local hospital – the mental ward, apparently.

I wasn't exactly sure what I was looking for. I knew there were mines on Granna's property; no mystery there, this was mining country. I had never heard of the Red Rover settlement, nor of any mine that had panned out in a big way. It was logical that archeologists would be interested in old mining camps. But why this mining camp? The Sierra Nevadas are sprinkled with abandoned mines and placers. I couldn't find a mention of the Red Rover in any book or article.

It was getting on towards lunch. I walked over to Royale House and bought one of their *Histories of Basking Township*.

"You're not taking the tour?" the girl at the counter inquired a little sardonically. She was tall and slender with long black hair, shiny as a raven's wing and beautiful sloe eyes. Part Indian, I thought. The Tuolumne Reservation was on the other side of the pine forest, and the Tule Reservation by Porterville was one of the largest in the state.

"What's the tour?"

"For three dollars you can walk through the house. Three stories. Count 'em, three." She pointed to a shelf of walkmans which must have taken the place of a decrepit tour guide. "For another two dollars you can have high tea on the patio."

Soggy egg salad sandwiches and tea from tea bags, if I knew my Historical Society high teas.

"Who were the Royales?"

She quoted, "In 1849, Abraham Royale came west to make his fortune in the gold fields." She paused to verify my rapt attention. "Abe wasn't much of a miner; however, he did manage to make his fortune by marrying the only daughter of a wealthy Chinese merchant. Unfortunately, polite society – such as it was in Basking in those days – would not accept the 'slant-eyed' daughter of a Chinese immigrant. Royale was an ambitious man. He traded in his Chinese bride, minus her dowry, for a local girl."

Something told me this was not the official version. "What happened to the Chinese bride?"

She smiled, her teeth very white. "There's no record. Probably died of a broken heart like all gently-reared girls of her era." So said the girl of this era.

"Tactful. What happened to Royale?"

"Ah. Now there's another story. Royale's golden-haired Anglo bride ran off with the smithy a year after their society wedding."

"Did Royale die of a broken heart?"

"No. They say –" her voice lowered dramatically "he died of the curse."

"Curse? What curse? Don't tell me the broken-hearted Chinese bride cursed him. What kind of gently-reared girl is that?"

She tucked a silky strand of black hair behind her ear. "To be honest, there are several stories. The only thing we know for sure is that Royale fell down the staircase right over there and broke his neck."

I turned to inspect the ornately carved grand staircase. Falling down that would be like tumbling down a cliff. I nodded towards the enormous portrait hanging over the marble fireplace.

"Is that Royale?"

"That's him."

At ten feet tall, Royale made an imposing figure. Dark hair, dark eyes and curling mustachios. A man cast in the heroic mould.

"One legend goes that he saw the ghost of his first wife and fell to his death."

"Is the house haunted?"

She shrugged. "Not that I've noticed. Not that I believe in ghosts."

Wow. How unstereotypical Native American.

As though reading my mind she added dryly, "Don't tell the tribal elders."

"Which tribe?"

"Miwok. Penutian Family. You really don't remember me, do you?"

"Should I?"

Her eyebrows rose. "I thought you were Anna English's grandson?"

"I am." When she didn't offer her hand I offered mine. "Adrien English."

"Melissa Smith. My father used to work for your grandmother. You locked me in the fruit cellar once."

"*I* did?"

I did sort of remember her now. She had been small, skinny and as irritating as a foxtail in your sock. "Not for long, I hope."

"I guess it was only a few minutes. It felt like hours."

"Sorry."

"I swore to get even, but you never came back."

"I scare easily."

"Don't worry, you're pretty low on my hit list these days."

If she was as tough at thirty-two as she had been at eight I hoped she didn't hold a grudge.

"I'm not up on local history."

Her dark eyes met mine. She smirked. "No, but you're making it."

I had a brief wait for Jake at the Bronco. I took a couple of headache tablets and washed them down with diet soda. At last I saw him come striding up the tree-lined street, in and out of shadows, big and purposeful. My heart did a little flip that had nothing to do with leaky valves.

I started the engine as Jake climbed in beside me.

"How did it go?" I questioned. "Were your fellow fuzz in a cooperative mood?"

Jake grunted. He drummed his fingers on the door armrest as I pulled out into the light traffic of Tuesday afternoon Main Street.

"Are we playing twenty questions or are you going to tell me what you found out?"

"The last time anyone saw Harvey was Thursday morning when he picked up groceries at the market up the street. He promised he'd be back the next day to pay his bill."

"But he was killed Thursday night."

"Maybe." He glanced at me. "Harvey has a girlfriend. He might be hiding out there."

"A girlfriend?"

I'm not sure why I sounded so amazed; probably because Harvey had been presented as such a loser by everyone I'd talked to. Jake said, "Most unmarried adult males do have girlfriends, Adrien."

I asked innocently, "Including you?"

Jake's eyes slid away from mine. He said, "The girlfriend might have a photo of Harvey or another lead."

"Doesn't Harvey have a police record? Aren't there mug shots I could look at?"

"Harvey has a couple of drug-related busts from the '70s. In those days he had long hair and a beard. I don't think a thirty second glimpse of a dead man in your headlights will make for an accurate ID."

He had that right. Already my memory of the man in the road was fading: imagination adding details, time erasing others.

I pulled up at Basking's one and only signal light, and said, "So where does Harvey's girlfriend live?"

Marnie Starr lived at 109 Oakridge Drive, a green tarpapered house at the top of a long flight of rickety stairs.

Marnie came to the door in a striped bathrobe, though it was past noon. A tall woman and built for comfort, she sized up Jake and me through the screen door mesh.

"Yes?"

"Marnie Starr?" Jake's stance, that official tone of voice, all spelled cop. I wondered if it was deliberate or something he couldn't help.

"That's right."

"I'm Detective Riordan." He nodded my way. "English."

"Detectives?" She stared at us through the cigarette smoke. She was about fifty, with long salt-and-pepper hair and freckled skin that had seen too much sun.

"May we come in?" Jake asked.

Automatically, she unlatched the screen and let us in.

The front room was small and cluttered. Copies of *The National Enquirer* littered the coffee table, headlines screaming alien abductions and movie star infidelities. The room smelled heavily of cigarettes and orchid air freshener.

"Sit down," Marnie said, gesturing uncertainly. "Detectives huh? If it's about the dog, I'm bringing him in at night now."

Jake sat down in a wooden rocker that creaked anxiously. I walked over to study a collection of framed photos on the TV.

"It's not about the dog," Jake said. "We're looking for Ted."

"Ted? Ted Harvey?"

"That's right. When was the last time you saw him?"

"Has something happened to Ted?"

"Why do you ask?"

"Well, if you are detectives..." she sketched the air with the cigarette. Jittery. Very jittery.

"We're looking for him, that's all, ma'am. When was the last time you saw Harvey?"

"Monday night."

"Last Monday night? You haven't seen him since?"

Her eyes fell. "Er – no."

"Did something happen Monday night?"

"No. No of course not."

I picked up a photo of Marnie in fatigues and a duck-billed hunting cap. She was holding a rifle. Behind this was another photo of Marnie and a slight, gray-haired man in a sailboat. I studied the man.

"Is this Ted?" I asked Marnie.

She jerked her head around. "Yeah, that's Ted."

Jake's eyes met mine. I nodded.

"What is this?" Marnie demanded suddenly. "You're not from the Sheriff's Department." She indicated me.

"I'm with LAPD," Jake answered briefly.

"LA..." Her voice gave out.

"What happened Sunday, Ms Starr? Did you and Ted fight?"

"It wasn't a fight. Not really."

"But you argued?"

Marnie seemed divided. At last she mumbled, "People say things when they're mad."

"What kinds of things?"

"I was just angry. I was sick of the promises and the excuses and the big talk. I'm fifty-three. No spring chicken. Is it so wrong to want a little security?"

I said, "You asked for a commitment?"

She turned towards me eagerly, as though at last someone spoke her language. "Yes."

"Did you threaten Ted?" Jake probed.

"Th-threaten? Not seriously. I mean, I love him."

"Uh huh. And how did Ted take this ultimatum?"

"He said he'd show me. That he was going to score big this time."

"What did he mean by that?" I asked.

She shrugged, stubbing out the cigarette. Then she dug in her bathrobe pocket for the pack. Her hands were shaking as she pulled another one out.

Jake said coolly, "Did Ted ever cheat on you, Ms Starr?"

She flushed so that her entire face was the colour of her freckles.

"No!"

"Did you threaten to kill him?"

"Who told you that?"

"Did you?"

"People say things when they're angry. It don't mean anything. Ted knew. Ted used to talk himself."

"Did he talk about his big score?" As I asked this question Jake shot me a warning look.

"No." She gestured vaguely. "What's to tell? He was just blowing smoke."

"Speaking of which, who's Harvey's buyer?" Jake took charge again.

"B-buyer?"

"You heard."

"I don't know what –"

"Skip it," said Jake. "We're just looking for Harvey. I don't care if he's wholesaling weed out of the back of his pickup."

"Why do you want him then?"

"Let's just say it's a matter of life and death."

She looked doubtful and I didn't blame her. I thought Jake should have come up with a better story than the truth.

We didn't get much further with Ms Starr. She took the card Jake handed her and said she would call if Ted showed. I had no doubt it sailed into the trash before we were down the ramshackle steps.

While Jake vacuumed up a late lunch, I moseyed on down to the corrals and, on impulse, went into the barn. Not that I actually expected to find marijuana drying from the rafters, but you never knew.

I entered through the tack room which still smelled of leather and liniment and sawdust. Bridles still hung from the walls. A saddle still waited for repair. I walked down the row of empty stalls. In my grandmother's day, the stable had been full of Arabian horses. Small-boned, fiery beauties with large liquidy eyes and graceful arched necks.

I'd had my own horse, a chestnut gelding I had named Flame (inappropriately, given his mild disposition). Flame had been sold with all the others following Granna's death, my mother Lisa fearing that I would break my scrawny neck.

Perhaps it was my father's early death that left Lisa so fearful about my own prospects. I was, as Lisa frequently pointed out, all she had. This was her own choice; Lisa made a lovely, rich young widow. Perhaps she had been afraid to trust her luck a second time around. In any case, Lisa had seen peril in everything from dogs to bicycles, and her worst fears seemed to have been confirmed when I contracted rheumatic fever at sixteen.

Now I stood in the empty stable breathing in the decaying memory of hay and horses and something bitter as wormwood. I recalled another of Lisa's strictures, the one about 'rough boys,' and grinned to myself as I thought of Jake. If ever anyone qualified as a rough boy, it would be Jake.

Wandering around, I had got to thinking of the old days and what a shame it was to let all this go to the termites and wood rot.

I could hear the buzz of insects. They sounded unnaturally loud. I looked over the gate of a stall. Something lay half-buried in the old hay and sawdust. Unlatching the gate, I walked into the stall.

As I stepped closer I could make out the outline, the pattern of material – plaid flannel.

My heart began to pound with revolted knowledge before my brain made the connection.

Within a foot of the thing I stared down and the buzzing of the flies matched the buzzing in my brain. I desperately wanted fresh air and light. I wanted to run from the barn and close the doors on what lay there in the mouldering hay. Close the door and lock it and forget about it.

The physical reality is so different from the academic puzzle.

I squatted down and brushed off pieces of straw.

The days had not been kind to him. But then again neither had been the person who shot to death Ted Harvey.

Seven

"It's not the same man."

Jake tore his gaze away from the official activity before us. The yard seemed full of black and whites, like a used police car sale. Men in uniform smoked and chatted – obviously a slow day for crime-busting in the Sierra Nevadas. "What are you talking about?"

"It's not the same man I found in the road that night. It's not Ted Harvey."

"Maybe it's not Ted Harvey but it has to be the same man."

"It's not." I broke off as we were joined by Sheriff Billingsly.

"I guess I owe you an apology, English," he said grudgingly.

"Yes and no. That's not the man I found in the road that night."

"Come again?"

"It's not the same –"

Jake interrupted in a tone of voice I hadn't heard since the first grim days of our acquaintanceship, "For Chrissake, Adrien, the guy is exactly how you described him, right down to the plaid shirt."

"Superficially, yes."

Billingsly looked from Jake to me and said, "You gotta admit, English, the chances of *two* different dead men turning up on your property are mighty suspicious."

Suspicious, not *coincidental*? Call me oversensitive, but my internal smoke alarms were going off. And where's there's smoke...

"Is it Ted Harvey?" Jake asked.

"Well no, it ain't," Billingsly admitted.

"Who the hell is it?"

The sheriff lifted his shoulders. "Don't know, but I'd sure like to have a word with old Ted."

We fell silent as the body was carried on a stretcher out of the barn and loaded into a station wagon marked Medical Examiner. The stable door was slammed shut by one of the deputies. Another began unrolling yellow crime scene tape to seal off the building.

Billingsly said, "Some place we can go and talk, English? I need to hear a little more about that night."

We trooped inside the house and Jake listened silently as I once again ran over my discovery of the body in the road. The sheriff took slow and copious notes, but he stopped when I tried to explain why I thought the body in the barn and the body in the road were two different men.

"The guy I found that night was more grizzled looking. Weathered. He hadn't shaved in a couple of days and his fingernails were dirty."

"You don't think the deceased in the barn looks battered enough?" the sheriff asked dryly. "Given the decomposition of the body, how the hell could you tell whether his fingernails were dirty or not?"

"I guess I'm not explaining this well."

Jake said forbearingly, "Adrien, you had a few seconds to run a make on a DB in the moonlight. It's been nearly five days. I think you are doing the normal thing, which is confusing that memory with the photo you saw of Harvey."

Billingsly interjected, "What photo?"

"I don't think so," I answered Jake. "When I saw this body, just for a minute I could see the first guy's face, like it was superimposed. This corpse didn't look at all how I remembered."

"It's been five days!"

"What photo of Harvey?"

"Adrien saw a snapshot of Harvey somewhere," Jake replied vaguely. "Keep in mind, Adrien, you are not a trained observer." Then, like a born and bred asshole, he added to the sheriff, "He writes murder mysteries."

Billingsly took a moment, sliding the beads across his cerebral abacus one by one. "Oh, I gotcha. Like *Murder She Wrote*!" He guffawed, the sound ricocheting off the hardwood floor and my nerves.

I tried to hide my irritation. "I admit my memory of the first body is fuzzy, but when I saw this man's face it struck me as wrong. I know my first impression was correct."

Billingsly at last containing his amusement, said, "English, you been through plenty, I give you that. Lots of material for stories, eh? You probably can't wait to get home to LA."

I sent Jake one of those poison pen looks. He met my eyes and glanced away, addressee unknown.

Billingsly made a few more notes, clearly humouring me. He then thanked me for my time and trouble, and took himself off. His was the last of the fleet of cop cars to leave my property.

When the sound of engines had died away, the kitchen seemed mighty quiet. The heavy, cool scent of just-bloomed lilacs drifted in the open window easing the memory of that other smell.

"That's that," Jake said, setting the coffee cups in the sink.

"Is it?"

"Yes." He turned to study me. "Don't start trying to make a

mystery out of a molehill. Your missing body has been found. The vic was probably a confederate of Harvey's. Harvey killed him and now he's split."

"Harvey is dead."

After a pause Jake turned on the faucet. Over the rush of water I heard him say, "Maybe he is by now, but that's not our problem."

"If you say so."

"Meaning?"

"Meaning that I may not be a trained observer but I'm not blind either. Two different men. Two different bodies." I held my fingers in the peace sign though I was feeling anything but peaceable. "Why doesn't anyone want to believe that?"

He threw me a chiding glance. "Now it's a conspiracy?"

"Come on, Jake, you know what I mean. Everybody is too eager to accept the obvious solution. I know why you are, but why is the sheriff?

Jake turned off the water. "Baby," he said finally and almost kindly. "You have too much imagination. That's good in a writer and bad in a – um – detective."

"I seem to remember you saying once that a good detective isn't afraid to use his imagination."

"Do you take notes on everything I say?" he inquired a little exasperatedly.

"There's so many contradictions it helps to keep track."

"Uh huh. Which reminds me. Aren't you supposed to be writing or something? Isn't that why you came up here? I haven't seen you write a word since I arrived."

"And that's another thing: that *Murder She Wrote* crack!"

"I didn't make that crack."

"You set me up for it."

Jake folded his arms across his chest like the Rock of Ages, refusing to cleft itself for me or anybody else.

I know when I'm wasting my breath. Off I went to the study. Initially I planned only to sulk, but after a few minutes I got bored and picked up the yellow pamphlet I'd purchased at the museum.

According to *Histories of Basking Township*, Basking was first settled in 1848 by an ex-Cavalry scout named Archibald Basking. Basking was also an artist and his sketches of Indians and Indian life hang in local museums like Royale House. Basking had moved on into the pages of history by 1860, but by then the gold rush was in full spate and Basking Township had a sizable population. Even when the gold rush ended in 1884 many citizens stayed on in other fields of enterprise. Basking survived and even flourished, unlike most of the 500 mining camps spawned during the gold rush which were now nothing more than crumbling foundations or faded names on sign posts.

Blah, blah, blah.

Every now and then I looked up out of my book and caught a glimpse of Jake outside the window hammering a broken shutter into place, taking his aggressions out. I was surprised he didn't just spit the nails into the wood like Popeye the Sailor Man. As he worked he whistled grimly around the nails clamped between his lips. When he finished with the shutter he set about repairing the fractured rose trellis.

Snips and snails and puppy dog tails.

I read on till about five. By that time Jake was in the shower where I could hear him swearing over the erratic water pressure and fluctuating temperatures. (Ah, the sounds of domestic bliss.)

I confess I was a little discouraged. By now Grace Latham would surely have found a torn scrap of an incriminating note or a bloody footprint or *something*. Detective work is not only easier in books, it's more fun.

And that's when I found my first clue. There, in smudgy print, was the name of the mine owned by Abraham Royale: the Red Rover.

I tossed the book aside.

In the front room I poured a couple of whiskeys from a twenty-year old bottle Jake had located in the back of the liquor cabinet. I downed mine watching the wind rake the winter grass like an unseen hand through the fur of a sleeping animal.

Jake appeared in the doorway combing back his damp hair. The sun had deepened the colour in his face and a bronze corduroy shirt made his eyes look almost gold.

"You'd better wait a few minutes," he told me. "There's no hot water."

I handed him his drink. He swallowed and sighed appreciatively.

"Get a lot done?" he questioned.

"Enough."

"Listen, just in case, if anybody mentions what happened here today, don't start in about believing the dead man in the barn was not the guy you found the night you arrived."

"Why?"

"Just do me a favour and keep your mouth shut."

"Since you ask so nicely, how can I refuse?"

He gave me that smile that was more of a grimace and said, "Please."

"Hey, the magic word." I clicked my glass against his and polished off my drink on the way to the bathroom.

There was no hot water for my shower so I made it fast. Even so, the bandage on the top of my head got soaked and fell off. I examined it, tossed it in the trash and hoped the tonsured look became me. At least it wasn't permanent. Yet. I inherited my mother's baby-fine dark hair, and plenty of it. As a matter of fact I needed a haircut even worse than I needed a shave. I was having a go at my forelock with a pair of nail scissors when Jake showed up in the doorway.

"You want another drink?" he inquired.

"No."

He observed me snipping away and said, "The better to see you with?"

"I don't get it."

"The kid. O'Reilly."

My hand jerked and I nearly put my eye out. "You're kidding, right?"

But Jake had already disappeared. From the other room I heard him blowing his nose like the war trumpet of a bull-moose.

I pulled on a semi-clean pair of Levi's and dug a blue denim workshirt out of the bottom of my Gladstone telling myself that the blue matched my eyes and the wrinkles matched the lines around them.

It was sunset by the time we reached Spaniard's Hollow. Against a fiery sky, the tents stood black like paper cut-outs illuminated from within by kerosene lamps glowing cozily like 19th-century lithophanes. The sound of voices drifted across as we parked with the other vehicles.

The nutty professors were all present and accounted for with the exception of Dr Livingston who had been unable to make it back to camp in time for the festivities. Dr Shoup did the honors, giving us the grand tour of the site.

Though the get-together had been Shoup's suggestion, his demeanor had thawed only slightly since our last encounter.

"The term 'archeology' refers to the systematic and methodical recovery of the material evidence of man's past life and culture. It is a *science*," he informed us as he led the way into a tent crowded with cardboard filing boxes and several long tables piled with miscellaneous artifacts: broken bottles turned purple with age, arrowheads, a rusted belt buckle.

Shoup paused in the lecture. When we didn't argue he continued, "Our understanding of the past gives us the knowledge to shape the future."

I watched Jake size up Dr Shoup, from the toe of his spit-polished boots to the crown of his khaki safari hat. I recognised the sardonic curve to Jake's mouth and looked forward to his commentary on the drive home.

"How many people do you have on staff?" he asked politely enough.

Dr Shoup said, "There are eight of us. On the weekends our volunteers pitch in. In the summer it will be different. The university sponsors an adult field school program."

"University?" The cop, always wanting the facts straight.

"Tuolumne Junior College," I supplied.

Dr Shoup paused long enough to show us the improbably named proton magnetometer, explaining that the data collected by magnetometer surveys would be processed by the college computers which would then produce a variety of detailed maps, profiles and three-dimensional views.

"Maximal information, minimal ground disturbance?" I suggested.

"Quite."

Jake met my eyes and arched his brows.

"We are professionals, Mr English. We do not rape and pillage the countryside as you imply."

Jake said, "Huh?"

"Have you found the Red Rover mine yet?" I inquired.

Dr Shoup's eyes narrowed. "Er – no. Not yet."

"How can that be?"

He bridled at this. "To begin with, we don't have the exact location."

"It's a giant hole in the ground, right? Maybe boarded up? How hard could that be to find? Besides, mines had to be registered or staked, right?"

"We know the general area, but not the exact location. It's only a matter of time."

Shoup explained that in order to reconstruct the site, a horizontal grid had been laid over the entire area. The object was to recover all items within the grid and place them in their related stratigraphic sections. He showed us grids, maps, a basic wall profile and the daily excavation notes.

"Everything is completely regulation."

Strictly regimental. I resisted the impulse to salute. "I'll take your word for it," I said.

"This mine worth a lot of money?" Jake asked.

"Certainly not. The mine played out long before the end of the gold rush. The Red Rover is strictly of historical and cultural significance." Shoup proceeded to explain why.

Kevin joined us as Jake's eyes were beginning to glaze. He looked good in khaki shorts and a rolled-sleeve denim shirt – like a big Boy Scout. He and Jake briefly acknowledged each other, then Kevin grinned at me and held up the crescent-bladed shovel he carried.

"Number one tool of the archeologist," he said undervoiced, with a nod at Shoup's back. "Equally useful for digging artifacts or shoveling through the bullshit."

Dinner in the main tent consisted of chili made of franks and beans, and cornbread. The flickering Coleman lanterns threw a cozy light over the faces gathered around the long table, several that I recognised from my first visit. It was warm in the tent, smelling of propane and damp earth. Jake and I were greeted like old friends as we squeezed in at the table.

"Coffee or box wine?" Bernice offered gaily.

Jake opted for the coffee and I had a plastic cup of boxed rosé.

"So what do you think of our operation?" Dr Marquez, on my left, inquired. His melancholy dark eyes met mine as though waiting to hear the worst.

"It seems like you have a very professional operation here." Even while I chafed over the thought of test pits, I couldn't help but respond to the energy and camaraderie around us.

"Dr Shoup has a great deal of field experience. He's... on loan, you could say, from UC Berkeley."

"I thought Dr Livingston was in charge here?"

"That's true."

"When does Livingston get back?"

He drained his coffee cup. "Late tonight or tomorrow."

"Is this what you do full-time?" I queried.

Marquez smiled that mournful smile. "I'm an instructor at the JC. Geography and zoology as well as anthropology." He sighed. "Diversity means job security these days. Or the closest thing to it."

On my other side, Jake was shovelling through his meal like a 49er, responding to Amy's overtures between mouthfuls. She related the amusing tale of how she had nearly blown my head off and Jake nearly choked laughing.

About midway through dinner, Melissa Smith showed up and we cleared a space at the table. She wedged in between Kevin and Dr Marquez and hailed fellow-well-met me.

"I didn't realise you were a member of this expedition," I said.

Her look informed me that there were many things I didn't know. "I'm working on my PhD in Anthropology." She shook her hair back from her face and accepted a plate from Bernice.

Kevin said, "I hear you had some excitement at your place today."

"What's that?" Dr Shoup looked alert.

"We found a dead body in the barn," Jake said. "Probably a vagrant."

"Yuck!" said Amy. "What was he doing in your barn?"

"How should anyone know what a vagrant might be doing?" Dr Shoup barked like a bad-tempered schnauzer. "Any more bright questions?"

Amy coloured the shade of her red thermal undershirt.

Kevin refilled my plastic cup with more box wine. I smiled thanks. Kevin smiled welcome. Jake kicked my ankle.

"Ouch."

"Sorry."

We were scrunched together pretty compactly at the long table.

Bernice said, "But aren't you the one who found a dead body last Thursday?"

"Adrien," Jake clarified. "Adrien's the one who finds the dead bodies."

"Yeah, well so far I haven't generated any."

"What's that?" Shoup's utensils clattered against his plate. He goggled at us.

Beside me, Jake went very still, the only person to understand my meaning. And considering the fact that Jake had killed in order to save my life – and had nearly lost his shield over it – it was a bitchy thing to say.

"Jake's a cop," I said. "He doesn't trust anybody."

"A cop?" Kevin repeated.

Was it my imagination or was there an uncomfortable silence?

"Now that must be interesting work," Dr Marquez said heartily.

"What kind of cop?" Kevin asked.

"Detective. Homicide." Jake's voice was flat. He resumed eating, intent on spearing every last bean on his plastic plate.

Another of those weird pauses. Melissa chuckled then and said, "Well well. Maybe we should ask Jake –"

"Smith, you know my feeling on the subject." Dr Shoup cut her off with force.

As I studied the faces around us, only Dr Shoup met my eyes. "If there's something going on here that I should know about –"

"There is n-not," Dr Shoup said with that small and revealing stammer.

"What about the weird noises? The chanting?"

Jake made a sound as though he had inhaled a bean.

"The hollow is haunted, you know," Melissa said slyly.

"Here it comes," Kevin said, "The legend of Big Foot."

"Don't be so quick to scoff at others' beliefs, O'Reilly," Dr Marquez said seriously.

"That's right," Amy said. "Melissa's people were here when yours were still scratching for potatoes in Ireland."

"What the hell does that have to do with anything?"

Amy's logic seemed to have confounded even her. She shrugged and popped a frank into her mouth.

"There are trees in this hollow older than your United States have been united," Melissa said. "Those juniper pines by the tarn are four *hundred* years old. The fucking insects inside them have a more complex civilization than your own."

"Language," Dr Marquez cautioned.

"Mountains are considered strong power points," Bernice put in, handing over a bag of peanut butter cookies. "Water is another. There's your argument for the hollow being a portal to the spirit world."

"Psychic archeology!" hooted Kevin.

"This hollow has long been held a sacred place by the indigenous peoples," Melissa said. "The pictographs on the rocks above us tell the story of guardian spirits."

"Poppycock!" Dr Shoup said. "Not another word about werewolves."

Since no one had mentioned werewolves Jake and I exchanged a look.

I inquired, "Did you say –?"

Kevin met my gaze and grimaced. "Ask Melissa about 'The Devouring.'"

I turned to Melissa. She was still smiling but there was something in her eyes. Something black and unfathomable.

"Do you want to hear a spooky campfire tale?"

"Do Boy Scouts like to be prepared?" I ignored Dr Shoup's obvious displeasure.

Melissa pushed back from the table and folded her arms comfortably, seemingly at ease in her role of storyteller. The rest of us fell silent and waited.

"According to the legends of my people, when the land and the water and the sky had been finished to his satisfaction, Coyote-man stabbed two sticks in the earth at all the places he had chosen for The People. Half of those sticks became men, half became women. It's a Creation legend." She shrugged.

"The little ones learn the story of how Lizard-man convinced Coyote-man that it would be better for The People to have fingers instead of paws, and that is why, ever since, Coyote has chased Lizard in the rocks. But there is another story. An older story."

As Melissa moved into the rhythm of her story, her eyes half-closed and her voice grew low. There wasn't a sound all down the long table.

"This is the story my grandfather told me. My grandfather was a shaman. A wise man. He knew many stories. The story he told me was that Coyote-man would not listen to Lizard-man, not at first telling, and so the first people who came to life were given claws and fangs. Claws and fangs." Melissa held up her hands, curving them as though to show long claws. She curled her lip in a silent snarl. You could have heard a pin drop.

"Perhaps Coyote-man wished these first people to look like himself. Perhaps he was mocking his brother, the Wolf. No one knows. Some say this first people came to be in the days of the Great Serpents whose footsteps shook the trees. Some say these beings were born into a world where mountains spouted flame, where the red lava bathed the earth in rivers of fire. Who can remember before the time of the storytellers? But it is true that these first people were so fierce that when they woke to life, they sprang upon each other and began to devour each other, man and woman.

"Like wolves in winter, so did the first people feel the ravening for flesh and blood. Too late, Coyote-man saw what he had done. He tried to stop it before all were devoured, but could save only five of these first ones, these First People. Yet, having saved them Coyote-man did not know what to do with them, for they were as much animal as human, and there were already all the animal spirits needed in this world. So he named them The Guardian and sent them to guard the door between the spirit world and this one, and if ever man should trespass too close to the gateway, The Guardian shall fall upon him, devour him and rend him limb from limb."

As though hypnotized, we all stared at Melissa as she finished in a kind of sing-song, "He turned them into the darkness. The darkness of the deepest water or the blackest night, the black of the tree bark, the black of fur, the black of loam that sucks the unwary footstep. You will know them by the darkness if you stray too deep in the heart of night. But even before you feel their fangs and claws, you will see their eyes shining bright in the darkness like amber, like a hornet's sting, like fool's gold."

Melissa trailed into silence. No one spoke.

At last Dr Marquez chuckled and said, "I'm afraid there are several – um – holes in that story, Smith."

Melissa laughed too, the spell broken. "It's just a legend. A story to keep small children from wandering too close to the caves."

Dr Shoup snapped out like broken chalk, "It's this kind of irresponsible babble about legends and folk tales which inspire dolts to dig up and cart off every removable artifact, utterly destroying the sanctity of a site."

"We call it the Schliemann Syndrome," Dr Marquez informed me.

"But if Heinrich Schliemann hadn't listened to and believed the old legends, he wouldn't have discovered Troy," I pointed out.

Dr Shoup barked, "Troy? Which Troy? Troy one or nine or zero? A little learning is a dangerous thing."

The party broke up sometime after ten o'clock. As we cut across the wet grass to the Bronco, Jake held his hand out for the keys.

My car, I drive. That's the way I see it, but Jake apparently loses points any time he permits another male to drive him, so I tossed him the keys. I'd had too much cheap wine anyway and my headache was coming back.

We had gone a mile down the dirt road when I said, "That was a stupid thing I said at dinner about you."

Jake grunted which could have signified 'You're forgiven' or 'fuck off'. After a moment he said, "But I wish you hadn't let it out that I was a cop."

"So you do think something is going on?"

"No. I find it... socially awkward."

We landed in a pothole and I grunted as though *my* suspension had taken the hit.

"*Were* you ever a Boy Scout?" Jake inquired, shifting gears.

"No."

"Your mother, I suppose."

Jake has never forgiven my mother for trying to get him fired during his investigation of me. They are neither of them the forgiving kind.

"Were you? A Boy Scout, I mean."

"Hell, I was an Eagle Scout."

"Figures."

It was then, like straight out of *The X-Files* – or one of Melissa's ghost stories – that something flew out of the darkness. Something with burning yellow eyes and outstretched claws, shrieking down upon us.

There was a thud that should have broken the windshield. I had a wild impression of horns, a razor-sharp beak and those glowing eyes.

"*Shit!*" Jake swerved hard.

The jeep went off the road. Jake tried to compensate but we slammed down in a rut, our heads grazing the ceiling. As though locked on train tracks, we headed straight for a massive oak. Jake stood on the brakes.

Instinctively, I threw my arm up so I don't know how the hell we missed the tree, but we scraped by, literally, twigs and branches scratching the sides and chassis of the Bronco. I banged hard against the side of the door despite the seat belts, and my arm went numb.

The next instant the jeep clambered back on to the road, tyres spinning and spitting gravel. Jake cut the engine. We were both breathing hard. He turned on the cab light.

"Okay?"

"Yeah."

"Sure?" He looked green in the overhead light.

I nodded, rubbing the feeling back into my arm. "Jesus, that was some driving, Jake."

He opened his door and got out, walking back towards where we had hit whatever it was.

I unsnapped my seat belt and followed.

When I caught him up, Jake was on one knee in the road, an owl flung out before him. It looked huge, the wingspan nearly six feet. It was still quivering.

"God damn it," Jake was saying. He spoke slowly as though in pain. "God damn it to hell. I couldn't miss it."

"It flew straight at the car. It's a wonder it didn't break the windshield."

"It's beautiful."

It was beautiful. The pale feathers were so perfect they looked hand-painted. I saw the little tufts that gave the illusion of horns. The fierce eyes were already filming over.

I put my hand on Jake's shoulder, squeezed it. He made no move.

I stared up. The mist turned the sky white behind the pines. All the world seemed blanketed in soft white silence. An owl, I thought, age-old harbinger of darkness and death. In Native American lore the owl is a bird of wisdom and divination – and still they are feared as omens of doom.

One thing for damn sure, in no myth or legend in the world does killing one bring good luck.

Jake shook his head as though clearing it and said, "Christ, what a shame to leave it out here for the scavengers. It ought to be stuffed or mounted, donated to some museum."

"We can put it in the Bronco if you want. Tomorrow I'll try to find a taxidermist."

He was silent. At last he shook his head and rose. "It's done," he said. "Forget it."

Eight

The next morning, Jake rose at the crack of dawn to go fishing. I declined his invitation, burrowing under my pillow and telling him I was going to buckle down and work on *Death for a Deadly Deed*.

At a more civilised hour, I took Jake's Acura and headed into Basking. But before I left the ranch, I placed a call to my ex-lover Mel, who happens to teach Film Studies at UC Berkeley.

Lucking out, I actually caught Mel in his office between classes. We chatted briefly and then I asked my favour, namely what did he know about Dr Daniel Shoup. I prompted him, "Mid-fifties, favours safari hats and Gestapo boots."

Mel thought it over and then laughed that husky laugh I remembered so well. "Like Stewart Granger in *King Solomon's Mines?*"

I knew he would think of that. "Or *Green Fire*."

That evoked memories of late nights cuddled on the couch, eating hot buttered popcorn and laughing our asses off at the worst movies in the world. Mel must have remembered, too. His voice grew warmer.

"What did you want to know? He's kind of an oddball, even for Berkeley."

"I'm not sure. Rumours, gossip, innuendo."

"Actually, there is a rumour connected with him. The kids call him Indiana Bones, by the way."

"Bless their hearts."

"Yes. Well, he came to us from the British Museum – at least, that's what everyone thought. It turns out the British Museum never heard of him."

"Seriously?"

"That's the word on campus."

"How reliable is the word?"

Another husky laugh. "Take it with a grain of salt. Although, the good doctor and the University did part ways a couple of months ago."

Aha!

Though I pressed for details, Mel had little useful information to add to that. He pointed out that the Archeology Department is a long way from Film Studies. Just as Berkeley is a long way from Los Angeles.

Before I rang off, he asked, "Are you taking care of yourself, Adrien?"

Kind of a sore subject between us. "Of course. Absolutely."

"Are you – ? Have you – ?"

Found someone? "Sort of," I said. "I'm involved." (It's involved.) "Are you still with Phil?" The boy wonder.

"Paul," Mel corrected gently. "And no. We split up. About a month ago."

"I'm sorry." No I wasn't. I never was a good loser.

After several hours of scattergun research I located a number of articles on the Miwok, including a couple which dealt with the creation legends. The People's tradition is of a world formed by half-human, half-animal spirit beings with supernatural powers. Confirming Melissa's tale, after Coyote-man made the world, he argued with Lizard-man over whether The People would have fingers or paws. But I could find nothing about a first race of man called The Guardian who were born with claws and whose job it was to protect the spirit world entrance from mortal man. Nowhere could I find any mention of 'The Devouring'.

Which didn't necessarily prove a thing. The library was small and its resources were limited. I was trying to verify an esoteric point of Indian legend. Still, it was interesting.

Another fact I found interesting if not useful: the Kuksu, whose mysterious art decorated the rocks above Spaniard's Hollow, was a secret society of the Miwok tribe. Melissa was a member of the Miwok tribe.

Now and then as I looked up from my reading, I caught the eyes of a rather odd little man sitting on the opposite side of the railings. It was hard not to catch his eyes because he appeared to be glaring at me.

The third time this happened, I gathered up my books and notes and moved to the other side of the library. Despite what Jake thinks, I really don't look for trouble. Soon I was immersed once more in the story of the Chinese in California. I began to understand Abraham Royale's dilemma as I read of the anti-Chinese movement and the story of the 'Caucasian Leagues.'

Royale had married for money, but he had also desired status, and his second-class citizen bride was a liability there. Had he returned the dowry with the wife? I doubted it. What had become of her, this long dead woman? My understanding of Chinese culture was based on movies mostly, but I figured she must have been disgraced. What were the options of a 19th-century woman who had been ruined, let alone a Chinese woman? Despite their part in building the railroads and their willingness to take on the jobs no one else wanted, the Chinese had been despised, even hated. The anti-Chinese movement culminated in 1880 with a proposed amendment to the California Constitution which would have prohibited employment of Chinese immigrants.

The battle is an eternal one, though the race, religion, sex or sexual orientation of those discriminated against changes regularly. Maybe man's need for a scapegoat is genetically programmed into him.

As I was mulling over this notion, I glanced up from my book to find the old man (and I kid you not, there was *dust* on the shoulders of his black...what was that, frock coat? The latest from the Goodwill Signature Line?) staring at me between the shelves of the nearest bookcase.

I looked hastily down at the printed page. What next? Could this possibly have anything to do with what was happening in Spaniard's Hollow? I mean, the old guy looked like he belonged in the 1800s, but I kind of doubted he was a physical manifestation of a guardian spirit. Despite the dust.

Eventually, he wandered away and I packed up my research materials and headed to the front desk only to find him there before me. Cravenly, I made a detour to the Featured Selection shelf, trying to look inconspicuous. I wasn't more than a few feet away so I knew I was not imagining it when I heard the man in black mutter something to the librarian about 'avowed homosexuals.'

Though I don't recall taking my vows, my ears pricked up. I randomly pulled a book from the nearest shelf: it was about harnessing the electrical power of your heart. The idea was that by concentrating on positive thoughts, one could actually alter the heart's rhythm, which would allow one to stay calm, cool and collected 'even in the midst of chaos.' That sounded promising. I could try putting it into effect immediately.

"... filthy sodomites... the wrath of God... the day of judgment..." The little man's voice rose and then fell as the librarian made shushing motions.

More hissing. More shushing.

Rumplestiltskin finally took himself off with one final razing look my way.

The librarian's cheeks were as pink as the rhinestones in her glasses when I reached the counter. I could see she was trying to decide whether or not ignoring the incident was the most tactful thing to do.

A little advice passed on from my mammy: when in doubt, smile. I smiled tentatively. The librarian's cheeks grew pinker still.

"I must apologise," she said stiffly, furiously stamping the inside covers of my stack of books. "The Reverend is a – a *conservative*." I watched her small fist punching book after book, like an android running amuck.

"Reverend?"

"The Reverend John Howdy."

"What denomination?"

"I believe he earned his doctorate of divinity through a correspondence school."

Church of the Sacred Stamp?

I took my books and hastened around the corner to Royale House, where I found Melissa organising a rack of picture postcards.

"You just missed Kevin," she informed me.

"That so? I thought I'd take the tour."

"It's your three dollars."

I paid my three dollars, lingering for a time before the glass case displaying the first Mrs Royale's traditional wedding headdress and gown. The fabulous silk robes embroidered in scarlet and gold were doll-sized – she couldn't have stood over four feet tall. How old had she been? Seventeen? Sixteen? Younger?

I checked out Royale's master bedroom which had a gigantic canopy bed that must have seemed like a boat to China Doll. There were sepia photos in silver frames on the bureau. I stepped over the velvet-covered restraints to get a closer look. I recognised one from my copy of *Histories of Basking Township*: Royale and his partner in the Red Rover mine, Barnabas Salt. Another photograph showed Royale formally posed with a blonde woman in a stiff-collared dress. The second wife? They both stood rigidly as all folks in those old tintypes do; it would be a mistake to read anything into their body language. On the other hand, she *had* split with the smithy before the wedding cake was stale.

I stepped back over the velvet ropes. He had done all right for himself, had Royale, by 19th-century standards. He had a mansion on the hill full of furniture that must have cost a fortune in his day, let alone in mine. There were Aubusson rugs and crystal chandeliers. At night he had rested his head on Irish linen, and in the morning he had breakfasted off Wedgwood.

I strolled down the hall. In Royale's study there was a collection of baskets in assorted shapes and sizes woven by Miwok and Pomo women. Some were decorated with feathers, some were tall and closely knit for food storage. Designs in the basket weave symbolised arrow points, deer feet or rattlesnake markings. The collection might not have existed in Royale's day; the beautiful and primitive baskets were possibly donated to the museum in the years following Royale's death.

The same could be true of the 'Indian Life' sketches by Archibald Basking decorating the walls. More Miwoks? I examined ink sketches of conical Indian houses; scroungy children playing with scroungy dogs; Indian women weaving baskets. A third drawing over the fireplace caught my attention: this depicted a tribal dance. Warriors gyrated around a bonfire, a few of the dancers were dressed in animal skins complete with the heads of their former owners: a bear, a white deer with antlers, a wolf.

I looked for the title. It read, *Medicine Dance*.

I went downstairs and located Melissa.

"Can I buy you lunch?"

She smirked. "Eat your heart out, Kevin."

"Sorry?"

"Kevin's got the hots for you, in case you haven't noticed."

"That picture in the upstairs study. The one titled *Medicine Dance*. Is that depicting the Kuksu?"

The smile died out of her dark eyes. "What do you know about the Kuksu?"

"Just what I've read."

"There's not much written."

"But I'm a voracious reader. Speaking of voracious... lunch?"

Reluctantly, Melissa laughed.

We found a coffeehouse down the street and ate the best tuna melts I've ever had in my life – either that or I was hungrier than usual. Melissa fell upon her meal with the enthusiasm of the Assyrian wolf upon the fold. I'd have put money on her in an eat-off against Jake.

Marnie Starr was our waitress. She did a double take when she spotted me and nearly spilled coffee on a customer, but by the time she reached our table she had regained her composure.

"How are you?" I asked.

"Fine. The special is meatloaf." She took our order, scratching at her pad with her pencil.

"Any word from Ted?"

"No." She looked up then, glaring. "There's a warrant out for his arrest, thanks to you."

"I can't take all the credit. Ted did his share."

Marnie gave me a long steady look like she was lining me up in her sights. She turned on her heels.

When she was out of earshot, Melissa queried, "Is this a writer's curiosity?"

"What's that?"

"All these questions."

"I'm just making conversation."

"Come on, I know you didn't ask me to lunch because you're interested in me. Are you researching a book?"

"How did you know I was a writer?"

"That's a silly question. There are no secrets in a small town. Everybody knows everything about you."

I raised my eyebrows.

She shrugged. "Small towns, small minds. Let's just say you're something new to talk about."

Trying to read her expression, I said, "I have to admit I'm curious about some things I've heard from Kevin. I can't help feeling responsible for anything that happens in Spaniard's Hollow."

Melissa did a creditable impression of the glowering face on a totem pole, finally pronouncing, "You cannot own the land. The land owns you."

"Are you referring to property taxes or something more spiritual?"

Marnie returned with our plates before Melissa could elucidate. I salted my french fries and Melissa checked under her rye bread as though expecting a bomb. Marnie returned with a pot of coffee and topped off our cups. She seemed to linger over her task. Eavesdropping?

When Marnie left us alone at last, Melissa said, "Nobody wants to admit it, but something's wrong at the site. Maybe there is a simple explanation, but Kevin's not the only one who's heard things and seen things. I have too."

"Like chanting? Tell me about that."

"I've heard it. It could have come from the wind through the caves on the mountain, but I'll tell you, it raised the hair on the back of my neck and I'm not easily spooked."

"What happened to Kevin's dog?"

"Blue? Coyotes, I guess."

"Is that what you think? Kevin said the dog was torn to pieces."

Melissa said slowly, "I'll tell you what I think. I think somebody doesn't want the past disturbed."

"Are we talking supernatural somebodies or somebody from around here?"

"I don't believe in ghosts," Melissa said.

"Do you believe in sabotage?"

There was a certain glint in her eye. "I don't *practice* it, if that's what you're asking."

"Do you believe The Guardian are protecting the hollow?"

She stared at me and said bitterly, "People mock what they don't understand. What they fear."

"I'm not mocking. I'm asking."

"I suppose you're not afraid either?"

I was saved from answering as Marnie brought the bill. I picked it up.

"No you don't," Melissa said, snatching for it. I held it out of her reach – old habits, I guess.

"Come on," I coaxed. "Let me see how it feels to be a chauvinist pig."

She eyed me narrowly but subsided. I never met a grad student who wasn't short of cash.

Melissa said, "Since you like legends so much, I'll tell you another about Abraham Royale."

"Yeah?"

"After his second wife ran off, Royale began to remember how faithful and obedient his first wife had been. He remembered her gentle ways and sweet smiles. He remembered her devotion to him expressed in a hundred little loving ways, and he went to San Francisco, to Chinatown, to find her."

Melissa paused. Looking up from figuring the tip, I nodded encouragement.

"Royale searched and searched but the girl's father had died. There was no other family. No one knew where Kei Li had gone to, though Royale questioned all the neighbors. He spent all that day hunting her. At last at nightfall he came to what seemed to be an abandoned house in the worst part of the city. He went inside, and to his amazement his wife was there, spinning away –"

"Spinning?"

"Well, whatever Chinese girls did during the day. Embroidering or working at a loom or something."

"Gotcha." I noticed Marnie was hovering again. Maybe she needed the table.

"Kei Li seemed to Abraham almost unchanged. As though not a day had passed since he left her at her father's doorstep. He stared and stared without the courage to speak. At last Kei Li looked up from her work and saw Royale who fell to his knees. He told her what a fool he had been, and how much he loved her, and how he had been searching for her high and low, and how she had always been in his thoughts, and how each night he dreamed of pillowing his head on the soft black silk of her hair." Melissa brushed the soft black silk of her own hair over her shoulder.

"And she said?"

"Kei Li wept and said she still loved Abraham and had prayed night and day that he would return." Melissa popped the last bite of dill pickle in her mouth. "So they went to bed –"

Crunch crunch.

"And?"

"And when Royale woke the next morning he found he was holding a skeleton with long black hair wrapped around his hands and throat.

She stopped as I chuckled.

"This sounds familiar. Like that Kobayashi movie, Kwaidan. The 'Black Hair' segment, I think."

Melissa eyed me consideringly and then burst out laughing. "You're the first person who ever caught that." She lifted a dismissive shoulder. "Anyway, it makes a good ghost story."

By the time I left Basking, the blue skies had turned grey and April showers were falling. The mountains were wreathed in cirrostratus clouds promising snow.

I figured Jake would have to cut short his fishing trip. I didn't know how long it would take him to get back because I didn't know how far he had travelled in pursuit of man's 'other favourite sport'.

Weighing the chances of getting snowed in with Jake, I had to wonder whether that would be a good thing. Not if we ran out of supplies, I concluded, with a glance at the paper sacks in the back seat. Lots of red meat, lots of cold beer: it was like feeding a lion with a drinking problem.

At the mouth of Stagecoach Road, I parked and got out to check the mailbox.

The rain was coming down hard now, everything green was

sombre and glistening. The scent of pine and wet earth filled my nostrils.

Rain was ticking on the mailbox as I opened the door.

I'm not sure what saved me. I heard something above the rattle of the rain: another rattle, a sizzling sound almost. I had an impression of motion inside the box, a couple of circulars moved. I yanked my hand away and jumped back.

The snake struck at the empty air.

As I stood there gaping, I recognised the distinct triangular-shaped head of a rattlesnake.

I backed up another foot or two, rubbing my hand, double-checking that I hadn't been bitten. I was so shocked I didn't even yell. The surprise was that my heart didn't give out then and there. In fact, once it started beating again, it was almost steady. Keep thinking those happy thoughts, I told myself, watching the rattler withdraw back into the junk mail of the mailbox. From its hiding place it watched me, its tongue flicking out.

I got back in Jake's car, found his phone and dialled for help.

In less than half an hour the now familiar black and white truck pulled up, giant tyres shelling gravel and mud. Billingsly and the ever present Dwayne fell out wearing yellow rain slickers.

"I might have known it was you," Billingsly said gloomily.

I explained the situation. As though it were perfectly common-place, Dwayne reached back in the cab and pulled out a long hook-like rod. In a few minutes they had the snake out of the mail-box and on the road where they promptly dispatched it. So much for the Save the Wildlife Fund.

Billingsly scratched his skunk-toned beard. "Just a little one," he reassured me, "though their bites can be the worst. The young 'uns don't know how to judge. They shoot you the whole damn dose."

"Kind of a weird thing, that snake in there," Dwayne observed to his chief.

"Yep, that is weird, although I've seen weirder. I remember one time –"

"You're not telling me you think this is a – a natural phenomenon!" I broke in.

Billingsly frowned at me. "What do you think it is, English?"

"I think someone put that snake in the mailbox."

He shook his head at my ignorance. "You be surprised at the places snakes crawl into. Dwayne had a snake wrapped around the towel bar in his john once."

"The *upstairs* john," Dwayne told me as though that should settle it.

I said exasperatedly, "A snake could not climb up into a mail box and shut the door after itself."

They stared at me. Rain dripped off the brim of Billingsly's hat. "So what is it you're suggesting? You think someone *deliberately* dropped that snake in there? Why? To bite somebody? Maybe the mailman? Or maybe you?"

I hadn't thought about the mailman, frankly.

"To bite me. Hell, I don't know! Maybe to scare me. I only know that snake didn't get in there by itself. Or by accident."

The sheriff said quite irately, "You know, nothing like this ever happened here before you came along."

"This is my fault?"

"I'm just calling 'em like I see 'em."

Swell.

I said as calmly as I could, "Thanks for your help. I take it you don't want to write a report or anything?"

Dwayne drawled, "Oh, we'll be writing a report."

I was already moving towards the car. Billingsly's next words froze me mid-step.

"Not so fast, English. We were coming to see you anyway."

I didn't like the sound of that. I didn't like standing here getting wetter and more chilled by the minute. I longed for the comfort and safety of home, my quiet little shop, my ordinary boring life where my biggest problem was if I was ever going to find someone to share my ordinary boring life.

"What's up?"

"We're trying to put a name to that dead body you found."

"Which one?"

He let that pass. "Missus Jimson at the general store says you told her Friday morning that you were expecting company that night. Now, I know it wasn't your buddy the cop, because I called him myself Saturday night. So where is this other guest of yours? What happened to him?"

My mouth dropped. I stood there, letting the rain in while I gaped.

"There wasn't one. I made him up."

Billingsly and his deputy exchanged a look and moved in – actually I think Billingsly only shifted his weight, but I was rattled.

"But surely..." My voice unexpectedly gave out and I had to try again. "The postmortem will tell you how long he's been dead."

"Yep."

Yep? What did that mean? Not that I was any expert, but the dead man looked as though he had been there a while. Longer than a week.

Good-bye to pride, good-bye to dignity. I babbled, "You've got to believe me. There was no one else. I said that because it's isolated up here. I said it in reflex. I was jumpy. I'm used to living in LA."

They stared as stolidly as the white-face beef cattle by the side

of the road. An effect heightened by Dwayne chomping his tobacco cud.

Billingsly said slowly, grimly, "You're one of them funny boys,
ain't you?"

It was hard to speak, what with my heart trying to climb out of
my mouth. For every gay man this question comes at some point,
in just such a tone, if not in those actual words. I don't know if
real courage lies in storming barricades or simply not denying the
truth. I know it took every ounce of strength I had to say, "I'm gay,
if that's what you're asking."

"Your pal, Riordan. He one, too?"

"You'll have to ask him."

Dwayne spat a stream of tobacco juice an inch from my boot.

They continued to stare at me.

Why wait for the law? Let's string him up! Except that they were
the law.

"I'll tell you flat, I don't trust you, English," Billingsly told me
flat.

"Listen," I said, "Why would I make a point out of the dead
man in the barn not being the same man I found Thursday night?
Why would I direct your attention to him if I'd killed him? Is that
smart? Is that logical?"

"How the hell do I know how smart and logical you are?"

Seeing that I didn't have an answer to that, Billingsly added, "I
done some checking. This ain't the first time you've been involved
in a homicide."

"A homocide," clarified Dwayne.

"Someone tried to kill *me*."

"That happens to you a lot."

"Okay, okay. What about the gun he was shot with? I don't own
a gun. You can search the place if you want."

I knew this was a mistake as the words left my mouth, but surprisingly the sheriff didn't jump at it. Indeed, he got a suspicious look on his face as though he'd just been dealt his fifth ace.

"Sure, you'd like that. Then you could sic your ACLU shysters on me."

"We could get a search warrant," Dwayne suggested. His ears and nose were turning red with cold. It felt like snow in the air.

Maybe the words froze in my throat. Or maybe I honestly couldn't think of anything to say. It doesn't happen often. I just stood there as though struck dumb.

Billingsly jabbed his finger my way for emphasis. "Don't even *think* about leaving town, English."

It was nearly five before Jake walked in. He was sunburnt, wet and smelled faintly of fish.

"The only thing worse than opera is someone who hums along with opera."

I stopped typing. "Turn it off."

Jake reached over my shoulder and turned off the CD player, cutting Bocelli off mid-high note.

In the silence I could hear rain drumming down on the roof.

"Get a lot done?"

"Sort of. Jake –" I started to turn in my chair.

He put his arms around me. "God, I'm starving." He pressed his mouth against my throat and growled from deep down in his own.

My nerves being a tad frayed, I jumped a foot and nearly clipped him under his chin. Jake let go of me and laughed.

"How about fish for dinner?"

Shit shit shit. The timing was all off. I was zigging, he was zagging.

"Fish is good if I don't have to clean it."

"I'll clean it," he said. "Hell, I'll even cook it if you take K.P."

"Deal."

Jake was heading back to the kitchen. I got up and followed him.

"Jake?"

He paused, his hand on the door to the yard.

"I – uh – there was a rattlesnake in the mailbox today."

He took it without blinking.

I ploughed on. "I called the sheriff and he didn't take it too seriously, but – well, Billingsly told me not to leave town."

"Told you not to leave town?"

"Right."

I was waiting for the nuclear reaction, the meltdown. Jake said very calmly, "That's bullshit. Unless he's actually charging you, no cop can order you not to leave town. What aren't you telling me?"

"I'm telling you now."

"Where's this mailbox?"

"On the highway."

"What were you doing on the highway?"

I tried to keep it light; offered a smile. "This feels like an interrogation."

"Why were you on the highway?" Crisp and clean and no caffeine.

"I drove into town to pick up some groceries and a copy of *Titus*." At his blank look I said, "*Titus Andronicus*. The play I'm basing –"

"You were playing detective."

"Not really, Jake."

"Yes, you were."

"Yeah, okay, maybe I was. Jake, I know you think that I'm imagining things –"

Jake walked out. The screen door swung shut behind him with just a suggestion of a bang.

*

"You'd better tell me what you found out," Jake said, pushing his plate away.

I had been staring down at my plate, holding the fishy eye of the trout lying there, when Jake deigned to speak. His voice startled me.

Dinner had been civil but strained. The food was good. Jake had fried up the fish, and made rice with garlic, cilantro and green onions. Someday he was going to make some woman a wonderful wife. I tossed together an unimaginative salad of spinach and wild lettuce, and uncorked the Clos du Bois, my favourite California wine. I thought it might cheer me up. Jake and I moved around each other in the big kitchen, not speaking except when he asked me where something was.

I got the silent treatment during the meal too. I didn't like it. It reminded me of the way Mel used to clam up when he was angry. I reacted by drinking too much.

I tossed my napkin over the remains of the fish. I said, "Suppose someone wanted to protect Spaniard's Hollow?"

"From?"

"Exploitation. Desecration? The hollow was considered a sacred place by the Kuksu."

"What's the Kuksu?"

I think it was Mark Twain who said, 'Get your facts straight, and then you can distort them as much as you like.'

"The Kuksu were a secret society of men and women, a religious cult whose members dressed in elaborate costumes representing ghosts or divinities."

"Impersonating the spirits of the dead?" Jake tilted back his chair, drained his glass. He was knocking the booze back himself.

"Right. The Kuksu are associated with the Miwok tribes. The Miwok are one of the predominate tribes in this area. That story Melissa told us last night is a Miwok creation legend. The Miwok call themselves The People. They're not the only tribe who do; the Navajo call themselves The People too, still..."

"Is there a point to this?"

"Melissa is a member of the Miwok."

Nothing from Jake.

I rushed on. "There's something else. When we were kids Melissa used to talk about going on rattlesnake hunts with her father. I know that's probably just a little kid bragging. I know it's circumstantial, but..."

Jack said impatiently, "It's hearsay. It's jack shit."

"Look, I'm not accusing her of anything. You asked what I found out." I decided to wait until later to tell Jake about my conversation with Mel.

"You think Melissa put the snake in the mailbox? Do you think she also killed the vagrant in the barn? Why?"

"I'm not saying that. I don't *want* to think Melissa is involved. I'm theorising. Maybe the two things are not connected. She doesn't know I've got a bad heart. Maybe the snake was only meant to scare. Those stories that she told last night sure were designed to scare. Everything that's happened at that camp has been designed to scare people off."

Jake was silent. He shook the ice in his whisky glass. It made a chilly angry sound. At last he spoke, his comment being, "How did you not get snake bit?"

"Luck. It was cold inside the metal box. I guess the snake was sluggish."

No comment.

"I'm not sure why you're pissed about this," I said.

"I'm not. I think you're in over your head."

"Fine, Jake, what do you think I should do? Go home to LA and forget it?"

His eyes narrowed.

Knowing it was a mistake I pressed on. "Is that what you would do?"

"You're not me."

"But that's what you think I should do?"

Some kind of internal struggle seemed to take place.

"Do you have a plan, Adrien? Or do you just intend to hang out here until someone puts a slug in you?"

Now there was a happy, positive thought to focus my heart's energy on.

"Do you understand that you could be arrested?"

I stared down at my empty glass. "I haven't done anything."

"Grow up, Adrien. For Chrissake! What's happening to you? You have a business to run. You have to earn a living, remember? You leave town without a word. You hide out here – have you bothered to check in with Angus since you got here? Have you bothered to find out if your shop is still standing? Have you even called your damn mother?"

"My *mother*?"

But Jake was on a roll. "You want my take? I don't know what you're doing up here, but it seems to me like you're hiding out from something."

"Well hell, Jake, you missed your calling. You should be a shrink not a detective."

Jake's chair slammed down on all fours. "Someone put a snake in your mailbox because you are going around asking questions. Do you get that? There's a direct correlation."

"Yeah, I get that," I returned caustically. "I'm surprised you point it out though, since according to you I'm making mysteries out of molehills."

Jake said shortly, "I'm going to bed."

Nine

When I woke the next morning, I could hear Jake snoring down the hall. Either that or he was taking a saw to the wall.

Stumbling into the bath, I relieved myself and paused at the apparition in the mirror. I'm a lumberjack and I'm okay? I looked like one of the legends I'd been reading about till three in the morning: the Blue Lake Monster or Sasquatch. I splashed cold water on my face, combed my wet hair back and shook out a pair of jeans.

In the kitchen I fried up bacon and put the coffee on.

Jake, lured by the smells – or the crash of the cup I dropped – wandered in wearing a pair of Levi's and nothing else, and dropped down at the table. He scratched his very flat, hard belly in a leisurely fashion, brooding. I put a cup of coffee in front of him. He leaned over the table, both hands clasping his coffee cup as though in prayer.

"Fried or scrambled?" I held up an egg.

"Scrambled."

I scrambled and said, "Listen, Jake. I thought over what you said last night. The fact is, you're right. I've decided to go back to LA."

Watching him out of the corner of my eye, I saw his head jerk up like Smokey the Bear scenting forest fire.

"I've got a few things to wind up and then I'm out of here."

A beat.

"You're serious?" he said finally.

"Yes."

Another beat. Jake drank some coffee, set the cup down and said more cheerfully, "Well hell, maybe I should head back today?"

"That's what I was thinking."

"You think that would be a good idea?"

"I do. In fact I'll be right on your heels."

He smiled. "Hey, I could pack and be on my way by lunch."

"You won't have to miss another day's work."

I stopped because Jake was laughing.

"Man, you are something else," he said shaking his head.

"I don't follow?"

"Spare me the little boy blue look," he said. "You're trying to get rid of me."

"No way. Really."

"Shut up, Adrien," he said. "I did some thinking myself last night."

He didn't say anything for a moment, then he admitted, "I was in a pisser of a mood at dinner."

"That so?"

"It was my birthday yesterday. I have a hard time with birthdays."

This was the last thing I expected. I mean, obviously Jake had birthdays like everyone else, but I guess it underlined how little I knew about him. Not the most basic things. Not his blood type. Not his birth date.

"Why didn't you say something?" I didn't like the tone of my voice but I couldn't help it.

Jake shrugged.

"How old are you?"

"The big 4-0. Forty." He grinned sheepishly.

Eight years older than me. And a Taurus. The bull. The bull-head. "Happy birthday," I said cordially and turned back to the stove.

The bacon popped and spat my way.

I heard a chair scrape. Jake came up behind me and wrapped his arms around me. Sniffing my ear, he said, "You smell good. What is that?"

"Bacon grease."

He grunted.

I could feel his body all down the length of my own; feel the hard muscles in his thighs and arms, feel the heat of him through our clothes.

"How about I let you treat me to dinner tonight?" Jake's breath was warm against my ear.

"I could take you to lunch and you could be home by nightfall."

"Nah," said Jake. "Today we're going to see what's up with our friends at the Red Rover mining camp."

It looked like a town meeting was in progress when we reached the hollow.

"You don't think – ?"

"I think," Jake said, opening his car door, "You need to decide what you're going to do about all this. Pron to."

Great. I didn't have a clue what I was going to do about all this.

Kevin detached himself from the crowd gathered around the supply tent, and strode across the grass to meet us.

"We found the entrance," he called.

Together we walked across the clearing while Kevin explained that the mouth to the Red Rover mine had been discovered a mile from base camp. Discussion raged as to whether camp should be moved or not.

Everyone but Melissa seemed to be there, and everyone seemed to have an opinion. Shoup and Kevin were all for pulling up stakes. Marquez led the others in loud objection.

"Isn't it up to Dr Livingston, anyway?" I suggested to Kevin undervoiced, while the opposing arguments were being made.

"Sure, if we could get hold of him."

"What does that mean?" Jake interrogated, in his cop voice.

Kevin shrugged. "He's not at his hotel, and he was due back two nights ago."

"He checked out?" I asked.

"That's just it. According to the hotel, he never checked in."

"Could the hotel have made a mistake?" I inquired out of bitter experience. The generator kicked on. I had to strain to hear Kevin over the rattle and hum of mechanical indigestion.

"Sure. That's probably it, but it doesn't change the fact that he's not here. No one at the JC has heard from him. His wife hasn't spoken to him in almost a week. She didn't know he had left the site."

Kevin was summoned away by Dr Shoup, who looked none too thrilled to spot Jake and me in the crowd.

I said to Jake, "Modern marriage, huh?"

"What's that?"

"The Livingstons."

He gave me one of those grunts that indicated he wasn't really listening, so I wandered over to Dr Marquez who seemed about as animated as I'd seen him.

"They don't know what they're asking," he said to me hotly. "All these file cabinets, all these boxes of artifacts, we can't just throw them in a truck!"

"What happens if you don't move the camp?"

"Nothing! It just means we have to walk further to and from our digging. It's an inconvenience, but not as much an inconvenience as picking up stakes and dragging everything down the road."

He studied me, a speculative gleam in his dark eyes. "You could refuse to let them move the campsite. It's your land."

"I'll pretend I didn't hear that. Can I see the mine?"

After a hesitation, he nodded. I caught Jake's eye and indicated where I was going. He nodded.

Marquez seemed disinclined to chat as we left the camp behind us and walked into the woods. I didn't take it personally; he was not a chatty guy.

"So what's this about Dr Livingston disappearing?" I asked as we followed the ruts of the old stage road. Grass and wildflowers covered the faint indentations, but the track was still there, leading straight into history.

Marquez paused mid-step. "Disappearing? What are you talking about?"

"Kevin said nobody's heard from him since he left here. He said that, according to the hotel, Livingston never checked in."

"That's not true. He's called several times." Marquez stopped dead. His dark eyes glared at me through the thick lenses. "The hotel lost track of his reservation. What's unusual about that?"

"Nothing, I guess." Marquez turned and led the way through the undergrowth. I said to his back, "So if Livingston's due back any minute, why not wait and let him make the decision of whether to move camp?"

I didn't think I was going to get an answer, but then Marquez halted again, turning to face me. "Why? I'll tell you why. Lawrence – Dr Shoup – isn't about to wait for Daniel to return. Maybe I'm talking out of turn, but it's no secret he wants the credit for this find. He's not going to want to share that. Not if he has a choice."

This was the longest speech I'd ever heard Marquez make. I wasn't quite sure I followed his reasoning, but he clearly believed what he was saying.

"Am I missing something? What does moving base camp have to do with who gets credit for finding an old mine?"

Nothing.

"A lost mine," Marquez corrected finally.

"Okay, a lost mine."

Marquez took a deep breath and said, "It probably doesn't make sense to you, but a find, a significant archeological find, can mean the difference – academically speaking – between life or death."

I ducked a tree branch as it swung back behind Marquez. "How does the Red Rover mine constitute a significant archeological find?"

He was silent.

He was right, it didn't make sense. "I can barely find a record that this mine existed. Why is its discovery significant?"

"It could be."

"Why?" I persisted.

Marquez said reluctantly, "Because Royale was a rich man when he died – and it didn't come from some wedding dowry."

I turned that notion over, held it up to the light. "You think the mine is still workable?"

"Probably not, but you never know." He smiled at me more cheerfully. "Nice for you, eh?"

Thar's gold in them hills!

I opened my mouth to pipe up with the first of my many doubts, but was distracted by Marquez who pointed to the hillside before us.

"There it is. That's the mine entrance."

Staring past Marquez I spotted the half-boarded opening of what appeared to be a cave in the hillside; chill air whispered out of its snaggle-toothed mouth. Saplings grew out of the hillside, concealing the timber frame of the mine. Easy to see how it had been missed for so long.

"Who found it?" I asked.

"Melissa. And Kevin."

"Has anyone been inside?"

"Not yet. It may not be safe." Marquez's glasses glinted blindly in the sunlight. "The stairs down appear to be rotted."

Leery, I walked up to the opening and peered inside through the slats. It was pitch black inside. I couldn't see anything. The breath of the mineshaft was cold and dank against my face. I ducked back out.

"Watch for snakes," Marquez warned. "We found a rattler in camp a couple of days ago. They're irritable this time of year. They're shedding their skins."

I turned to stare at him. "What happened to the snake?"

"Dr Shoup killed it and buried it."

A thought went through my head – and kept on going. I just couldn't picture Indiana Bones tucking baby rattlesnakes in among the circular fliers of my post. And yet someone had.

"Are you sure this is the right mine?" I inquired as we started back to camp.

Mid-step Marquez paused. He gazed at me as though he suspected I was trying to be funny. "It's the only mine," he said with finality.

That night we celebrated Jake's birthday dinner at La Chouette, a century-old, two-story Victorian with a wisteria-framed verandah and a Parisian-trained chef.

"French food?" Jake said doubtfully. "What is that? Sauces and snails?"

"According to the Auto Club, it's the best place in town."

He mulled this over. "So long as I don't have to wear a tie," he conceded at last, grudgingly.

Neither of us wore ties. In fact we wore Levi's which were all we had, Jake complementing his with a tight black turtleneck that looked so sexy he could have modelled for the *Under Gear* catalog.

We kicked off the celebration with drinks in the cozy saloon-bar and then moved out on to the verandah for dinner. It was a lovely, mild evening, the outside heaters working overtime to keep it that way. Lost mines, rattlesnakes and dead bodies all seemed like something that happened to other people in distant galaxies.

"How's your book coming?" Jake inquired, making civilised conversation halfway through his *Delice de Veau*.

"It's coming," I said gamely, reaching for the thirty-dollar bottle of Merlot. "What were all those phone calls you were making this afternoon?"

"Just checking on a couple of ideas."

"Like?"

He pushed his glass my way. I filled it and signalled the waiter for another bottle.

I expected Jake to brush me off, tell me not to worry my pretty little head, but he said finally, "The problem is we don't have an ID for your stinker in the barn. Most homicides are solved within 48 hours, because most of the time there is a known connection between the perp and vic." He explained, "Cops ask themselves what would someone have to gain by the vic's death? Who profits? But if we don't know the vic, it's hard to draw a connection."

"We know about Ted Harvey."

Jake sighed but apparently decided to let it ride.

I swallowed a forkful of my *coq au vin*, and proposed, "Suppose Harvey's death has nothing to do with drug running?"

He mulled this over. "Your supposition is based on what?"

"On the fact that someone was searching Harvey's trailer."

"I'm not tracking."

"What would they be searching for?"

"Harvey," Jake said unhesitatingly. "Or money. What do you think they were searching for?"

"Jake, if we were dealing with drug runners don't you think their approach would be more direct? Do drug lords typically waste time playing with snakes and knocking people out? Wouldn't they just come in with automatic weapons and mow us down?"

"You've seen way too many Steven Seagal movies."

I choked on my wine. "Whose fault is that? Besides, Jake, I think handling a rattlesnake demands a certain amount of expertise. You don't just buy them at pet stores. You have to find one, first off."

"Maybe."

"What do we know about Harvey? He was a doper, yes, but he was also a small-time crook not above trying his hand at fraud. Maybe he got ambitious."

"You think Harvey did the DB in the barn?"

I moved the candle aside to see his face better. "I don't know. But you heard Marnie Starr say Harvey was boasting about a big score. What does that sound like?"

"A drug deal."

"Forget about the pot for a minute," I said, nettled. "What *else* does it sound like?"

"What?"

I pushed my dish out of the way. "That's what we have to figure out."

Jake shook his head a little and carved another hunk off his veal.

"I've been thinking about that corpse in the barn," I said.

"I don't doubt it."

"It's a small town. How come nobody has claimed him?"

"Maybe he's not from around here."

"Then how did he get here? Where's his car? The sheriff must have checked against missing person reports."

"I'm sure you've got a theory."

"Maybe no one knows he's missing yet."

A busboy whisked away my plate. I leaned forward on my elbows. "Maybe no one knows he's missing because until today everyone thought they knew where he was," I offered.

Jake looked up then, his expression wry. "Dr Livingston, I presume?"

"You think it's crazy?"

He floored me by saying, "No. The thought occurred to me today, too. I guess we ought to have Billingsly get someone from the site to take a look at John Doe."

The waiter brought the dessert tray and Jake selected a white and dark chocolate mousse with raspberry sauce. I ordered the Hot Brandy Flip which turned out to be three parts brandy and one part flip. A couple of swigs and I started wondering if Jake's mouth would taste like dark chocolate or raspberry?

To distract myself from my incredibly shrinking jeans, I questioned, "So what's the deal with turning forty?"

Jake shrugged.

"You thought you'd be a lieutenant by now?"

"Nah." He met my eyes briefly. "I just thought I'd be... I don't know."

I made a wild guess. "Married?"

His eyes met mine. "Yeah, maybe. I guess I expected to have kids by now. My own family."

"Kids?" I echoed.

He said defensively, "I like kids. I'm good with kids."

"You are?"

"I've got nieces and nephews."

Jake's biological clock was ticking. Who'd a thunk it? I sighed.

"Okay, I'll do it. I'll have your baby."

He stared at me, unamused.

"It's a joke," I explained. "The truth is, I can't have babies. My doctor told me."

"See, you say I don't communicate, but when I do..."

Damn. A billy club right between the eyes. I blinked at him a couple of times. "Sorry," I said. "I guess I don't get it."

His eyes looked amber in the candlelight. "You don't care that you will never have kids? Your family line ends with you?"

"Probably a wise decision, don't you think?" At his expression I admitted, "Oh, hell. I'm not the paternal kind. Kids make me nervous. Kids and little dogs."

Jake finished his wine. The delicate crystal stem looked effete in his large, tanned hand. It was a hand designed for beer bottles and boxing gloves.

"So why don't you get married?"

He said finally, "I plan to."

Razors to my wounded heart, as Will put it in *Titus*. I drained my brandy and inquired, "Anyone I know?"

He probably would not have answered anyway, but right then the waiter brought the bill. I reached for the little leather book.

"Thanks for dinner," Jake said.

"My pleasure," says I.

We were passing the old movie revival house when I spotted the marquee.

"Hey, they're playing *Captain Blood*," I said. "We could catch the ten o'clock showing."

Jake, who hadn't spoken since we left the restaurant, said, "What is *Captain Blood?* Tell me it's not another pirate movie."

"You'll love it. It's got Erroll Flynn, your favourite not gay actor."

"What is it with you and pirates?"

"I don't know. My deep and abiding love of the ocean, I guess."

"Oh, what the hell," grumbled Jake and we pulled in the parking lot behind the theatre, Jake no doubt hoping to prevent any further spilling of conversational guts.

The theatre smelled of old popcorn. The red velvet furnishings were as tacky as the Coke-stained floor, but the seats were Jake-sized and comfortable, and it was all ours, except for the row of teens making out in the back.

For 119 minutes we lost ourselves in the black and white swash-buckling romance of 1935's *Captain Blood*, starring Flynn and Olivia de Havilland, who early on proclaims herself familiar with pirates and their 'wicked ways: cruelle and eville...' At which point Jake, his carcass arranged so as *not* to touch mine at any poten-tially interlocking body part, snorted and offered his popcorn.

It was a long drive home for a man who hadn't slept in two nights. Luckily Jake wasn't someone who required bright conversation to stay sharp. I woke with a crick in my neck as we were bouncing down the road to the ranch.

"Sorry. Was I snoring?" Gingerly, I swivelled my neck.

"It's more of a droning."

At least I wasn't drooling. I straightened up in the cramped seat.

We pulled into the front yard. Jake parked and we got out into the frigid night air. The wind blowing off the distant mountains tasted of snow. The clouds had cleared and the sky was brilliant with stars. The porch light spilled out over the steps and front yard.

When it happened we were walking towards the house; I was slightly ahead of Jake who was jingling the car keys in his hand. Something cracked past my ear followed by a bang that echoed through the mountains.

Behind me Jake uttered an oath, and the next I knew I was hitting the ground. Hard. There's nothing like being tackled when you're not prepared. And so much for all those Tai Chi exercises and instructions about sliding your palms and bending your elbows. I slammed down, the wind knocked out of me, with Jake on top. A second rifle shot split the night. The sound seemed to ricochet around the deserted ranch yard, rolling on forever.

I was trying to work out what was happening when Jake raised himself off me and fired his 9mm over my head. This took out the cheerful welcoming porch light.

"Move," Jake yelled in my ear. I could only hear him muffledly, due to the fact that I was half-deaf from the blast of the revolver a couple of inches from my eardrum.

Jake rolled off me and I got to my feet, sort of, and did a four-limbed running scramble for the porch steps. Not more than a hundred yards, but it felt like the LA marathon – or a gauntlet.

Every second I expected to feel bullets thud into my body, tearing muscle, bone, vital organs. There's nothing more frightening than being shot at (except maybe having a knife held at your throat).

As I reached the porch there was another shot. Jake, right on my heels, grunted and then yelled, "Stay low."

Yeah, no kidding. I had my keys out, though I didn't remember fumbling for them. I knelt down in front of the door, jamming one key after another into the damn lock until I found the right one.

More shots. One hit the porch post behind us. The other rang off one of the cowbells hanging from the homemade chimes in the pine.

I pushed the door open and Jake shoved me into the room and slammed the door behind us.

No more shots. Just the sound of our panting filling the long room. Tree branches scratched against the outside walls, the house creaked.

"Why didn't you fire back?" I gasped between breaths.

"He's got a rifle, probably with a scope. I've got a handgun. He could be half a mile away." Jake scooted over towards the window, a bulky shadow in the unlit room.

"Can you see anything?"

"No."

We waited while the wind moaned down the chimney. Jake muttered, "If he's got any brains he's halfway back to town."

"Town or camp?"

"Good point."

Jake stood, keeping clear of the window and yanked shut the heavy drapes, cutting off any outside view of the room. I did the same on my side. When the room was secured Jake said, "Okay, turn on a lamp. But – Adrien?"

"Yeah?" I paused, my hand on the switch.

"Don't freak. I've been hit."

"*What?*" I snapped on the light.

Jake was on his feet, and sure enough, his left sleeve was soaked with something darker than the black knit material. Something that glistened in the gentle lamplight. The blood trickled down his hand, which he was wiping on his jeans.

"It looks worse than it is."

"Sure, just a flesh wound," I said stupidly.

"It *is* just a flesh wound." Jake gave me a sharp look. "You're not going to pass out, are you?"

I shook my head.

"Because you're sheet-white."

"Just my girlish complexion." I got a grip on myself and said, "We've got to get you to a doctor."

"No. What kind of first aid kit do you have around here?"

"You're going to a hospital, Jake," I said. "I'm not in the mood to play doctor."

"For this little scratch?" Jake set his gun on the table and began struggling with his shirt.

I tore my eyes away from the Berreta. "You're damn right! You could get blood poisoning or lead poisoning or lose too much blood."

There was such a lot of blood. Blood smeared his breast and spilled out of the ugly ploughed flesh of his upper arm, in a slow but steady trickle. A fat drop hit the floor and splattered. The sight of it oxidised my brain.

"You're going to the hospital *now*." I headed for the door and Jake, half in and half out of his shirt, intercepted me.

"Hold on. Maybe you're right, but let's do this by the book. We've got to make sure he's gone."

"He's gone! He's not going to come after us. He knows you've got a gun. We've got a phone. He'll think we've called the sheriff."

Why the hell *weren't* we calling the sheriff?

"Let's do this by the book," Jake repeated. "We'll go for the Bronco, it's closer. Got your keys?"

I held my keys up. They were shaking. I lowered them.

Jake returned to the window. He parted the drapes a crack and stood motionless, holding his injured arm.

It felt like forever before he gave me a twisty smile and said,

"Stand by for action."

I opened the door. Injured or not, Jake moved fast. He brushed by me, and was out the door first. If I had been on my own, nothing on earth would have got me outside. I'd have stayed put and called for the cavalry, but no way was Jake going out there without me. I followed him out on to the porch.

Nothing moved in the yard. The wind rippled through the waves of grass and wildflowers beyond.

"Stay low, stick to cover," Jake instructed. "Give me the keys."

"You can't drive."

"I'm going first." As I opened my mouth to argue he plucked the keys out of my unresisting fingers and slipped out into the windswept darkness.

I followed Jake along the porch. He climbed over the rail and dropped down to the ground. I followed suit, hitting the hard-packed dirt with a thud that jarred my shins.

I imitated Jake's awkward running crouch to the old water trough. We were still a few feet from the Bronco. Jake motioned me to stay put.

Waiting, I broke out in cold sweat while he sprinted across the open space and ducked behind the Bronco tyre.

Silence.

The wind sighed through the leaves.

Jake got the Bronco unlocked. He slipped in. I heard the engine roar into life. I saw Jake's bulk slide past the wheel.

It was now or never. I'd have preferred never, but that wasn't an option. Hauling ass across the lot, I jumped in and slammed shut the door. My hands were shaking as I threw the gears into reverse and we shot back in a wide arc, just missing the tree with its swing gently swaying in the breeze.

"Easy, easy," cautioned Jake.

I cranked it into first and we tore out of the yard like the start-ing moments of NASCAR. The Bronco's tyres burned up the dirt road; we rattled across the cattle guard, bouncing down hard on every rut and rivulet in the road as we raced for the main highway.

"Shit, I'm getting blood all over your upholstery."

"I don't give a fuck about the upholstery!"

"I know, baby. Keep it together."

Second Action Figure not included. When I thought I could match Jake's neutral tone, I said, "Do we call the sheriff when we get to town?"

"Not unless you want to spend the rest of the night answering questions. There's nothing Billingsly can do tonight. Tomorrow I'll have a look for shell casings."

He grunted in pain as we hit a pothole.

"Sorry. Are you sure you're not –"

"The bullet nicked the fleshy part of my forearm." He tried to examine himself in the darkness. "I'm not saying it doesn't hurt like hell."

"I am so goddamn sorry, Jake."

"Knock it off," he growled. "It's not your fault."

"It is. If I hadn't insisted –"

"Shut up."

I shut up. Just as well. I had to concentrate on my driving since I was doing seventy on a winding mountain road.

Thirty minutes before, I had been so tired I didn't think I could stay awake long enough to walk to the bedroom. Now I was on an adrenaline rush that felt like it would carry me into next week.

The road snaked though the silent forest as I decelerated into each curve, accelerated out, the tyres squealing now and then when I turned the wheel too tightly.

Jake said nothing, his hand clamped over his arm.

I slowed to a sedate sixty as we tore through town, stopping at the twenty-four hour 'doctor in a box.'

We were the only customers past midnight. Jake calmly explained to the nurse behind the counter what had happened while little drops of his blood pooled slowly on the Formica. I hovered anxiously.

"Gunshot!" the nurse exclaimed. "We have to report gunshot wounds."

"That's not a problem," Jake said. He pulled out his wallet, but it was his insurance card he was after, not his LAPD ID.

The nurse shepherded Jake off to 'room number nine,' and I dropped down in an orange plastic chair in the empty waiting room, feeling like someone had yanked my plug. Like I couldn't have moved if my life had depended on it.

A few minutes later I saw a white-coated doctor go into room number nine and close the door.

How long did I sit there petrifying in the orange plastic chair? It began to seem like a very long time. Too long. Not only was I the only person in the waiting room, I seemed to be the only person in the clinic.

At last a door opened at the far end of the corridor.

A doctor I hadn't seen before was walking towards me. He was dressed in surgical scrubs and his face looked weary and grim. It seemed like he was walking in slow motion. My heart began to slug against my breastbone.

I stood up instinctively.

"I'm sorry," the surgeon said. "We did everything we could."

I couldn't believe it. I stood there my heart banging like a battering ram against a drawbridge. My body seemed to turn hot and cold by turns.

"That can't be right," I said stupidly.

"I'm sorry."

"But it was just a flesh wound."

"Guys like Jake always say it's a flesh wound."

"But –"

"He went into shock and we lost him. It happens."

I couldn't think of anything to say. I thought probably I was going into shock, too. It all began to seem far away, the hospital corridor receding, the bright overhead lights dimming, swirling away...

Ten

"Adrien."

Someone was shaking my shoulder.

I opened my eyes. Jake loomed over me, frowning.

My heart kicked into overdrive.

I croaked out some sound and leaned forward, holding my sides to keep my heart from bursting through my rib cage like the parasite in *Alien*.

Jake demanded, "What's the matter? What's wrong?"

I shook my head, unable to speak.

He began feeling around my shirt pockets. Irritating. I sucked air into my lungs, pushed his hand away and sat up.

"Hey," Jake said. "Are you okay? Adrien?"

The strange doctor, his bizarre comments – of course it had been a dream.

"I'm okay," I managed. My heart was staggering along, punch drunk and swinging wildly, but still in the fight.

"What happened?"

Under other circumstances the concern in his eyes would have cheered me no end. Now I snapped, "Nothing. Reaction."

Jake was alive. His arm was bandaged, a neat cuff of white around his muscular forearm. Otherwise he looked A-okay. I scrubbed my face with my hands, took another long cautious breath. Everything seemed fully operational again, but the dream had been so real that I still felt shocked and disorientated. Grieved.

"Here."

Jake reappeared at my side with a little paper cup of water from the cooler.

I got my pills out, popped the cap with my thumb and tossed two back for safety's sake. I took the cup from Jake. The paper felt squishy, too flimsy to contain the weight of the water – kind of how I felt. Like I could tear apart at the slightest pressure.

If something happens to him because of me...

If something happens to him...

"Are you sure you're okay?"

"I'm fine," I said impatiently. "How's your arm?"

"Kinda stiff. Funny thing: usually bullets bounce off me." He smiled a rare smile.

To make a long story short we ended up checking into the Motel 6, neither of us up to fending off another gun fight that night.

There's something safe and sane about the generic comforts of a budget motel chain, even when you wind up with the room by the ice machine. One room with one king-size bed. The walls were decorated with insipid watercolours of villas in the south of France for travellers whose idea of a dream vacation spot was Branson, Missouri. All I cared about was the deadbolt and chain decorating the door.

I slid the deadbolt, hooked the chain and peered out the peep-hole. Nary a gunman lurked in the parking lot.

"Cable," Jake approved, switching on the TV.

Heading for the john, I turned the sink taps on full and proceeded to lose what remained of my expensive dinner. When the dry heaves were over, I splashed a couple of gallons of cold water on my face and brushed my teeth with the toothbrush supplied at no extra charge by the front desk.

Stepping out of the bathroom, I found find Jake comfortably sprawled across the bed, propped up by pillows, remote control in hand. He was watching *The Hunted*.

"I'm not going to say I told you so," he remarked, as I tottered towards the bed.

"I appreciate that," I said. I lifted my side of the blankets. He was wearing black briefs. His body looked as hard and sculpted as one of those underwear mannequins in department store displays.

"If it's any comfort to you, I'd say we're on the right track. Tonight's ambush proves it."

Flopping back on the bed, I moaned with relief. Clean sheets – short sheets – but clean. Jake grunted and shoved one of the flat, spongy pillows my way.

"Next vacation, I'm going to Brittany," I informed him. "I've always wanted to go to Brittany." It sounded so safe, so civilised. Belle-Ile-en-Mer. Saint Brieuc. "I don't think they have guns in Brittany."

"That's right," approved Jake. "Why stop at pissing off local law enforcement when you can get the Justice Department involved?"

I balled the pillow behind my head. It was weird lying next to him, feeling the sheets heated by his body. He took up a lot of space. If I stretched out my leg I could run my cold foot down his hairy calf. I studied his profile.

Considering how long I'd waited for such an opportunity, you'd have thought I'd jump the big man's bones, but sad truth, I couldn't have got it up to save my life.

"TV bother you?"

I shook my head and closed my eyes lulled by the slashing of a thousand swords. One thing I don't fear is a ninja attack. Although the way things were going...

Dozing, I worked Jake's dour commentary on the movie into my nap. I was vaguely aware when he snapped out the bedside light. I opened my eyes. The TV screen flickered in the darkness with images of gore and, more frighteningly, Christopher Lambert's slightly crossed gaze.

Jake reached out, patting my face as though he were clumsily brailling me. I mumbled drowsily, and felt him ruffle my hair.

"You're not going to die in your sleep or anything, are you?"

"You'll be the first to know."

He laughed and tugged me his way. I can't say I put up much of a fight, rolling so that we lay against each other, chest to chest, cock to cock. Yep, it felt pretty comfortable even with my face smooshed in his armpit.

"Poor baby," Jake commented, his voice rumbling in his chest. He returned to watching his movie.

What the hell? I put my arm around him. No objection from Jake. His skin felt smooth, the blond hair crackled against my skin. He smelled of antiseptic and Jake.

My eyelids felt weighted. Listening to the reassuring thud of his heart, I let my body go slack and fell asleep in the crook of Jake's arm.

I woke with a boner the size of a small torpedo. For a while I lay there and watched Jake sleep in the early morning light.

In sleep his face appeared younger, the line of his mouth soft. I studied the white gauze bandage around his muscular forearm. I remembered Jake telling me big arms and shoulders were a help to a cop; a deterrent to punks and drunks who would think twice about taking on someone who was obviously in great shape, who worked out regularly.

Jake was in great shape, he worked out regularly, but one well-placed bullet last night would have ended his life. I guess until Jake was the one at risk I hadn't taken the threat to us too seriously. Not that I thought I was invulnerable; just the opposite. When you live with a potentially life-threatening condition, you get used to the thought of dying. You accept it, you push on. The thing that scared me was the picture of dying slowly and painfully, the loss of independence and identity to illness.

Or so I had thought until last night. Now I realised that I was even more afraid of something happening to Jake. He seemed so tough, so capable, but he was human, he was vulnerable. He could be injured, he could die. Maybe it was naive that this thought hadn't struck me until a bullet struck Jake, but there you have it. And all the jokes in the world about being bullet-proof didn't help.

Frowning in his sleep, Jake burrowed his face more comfortably in the pillow. I wanted to wrap my arms around him and reassure myself that he was safe and alive. Instead I edged out of the bed and headed for the shower.

By the time I finished shaving, Jake was sprawled on his back, arms outstretched, taking up 80% of the king-size bed, being a king-size guy. I sat down on the edge of the mattress, rolling my socks up.

I started as Jake ran a warm hand down my bare back.

"Morning," I said, turning to inspect him.

"Morning."

"How's your arm?"

"Sore." He smiled faintly, slid his hand down my arm. His fingers encircled my wrist, his thumb stroking my pulse point.

I warned myself not to get too worked up. "What did you do with your prescription? I'll get it filled for you."

Jake tugged my supporting arm and I let myself topple on top of him. He was still smiling, but his eyes were intent.

I tried to think of something clever to say.

Jake's mouth touched mine and it went through my mind that it was his first man-to-man kiss. I seemed to experience that kiss through Jake's virgin senses: the queerness of a man's hard jaw, a man's lips, the texture of a man's smooth shaven cheek, so different from a woman's soft skin. The taste of a man's mouth.

It was a tentative kiss, a first kiss. The second kiss was not tentative, and I did not experience it through Jake's senses because my own were swimming.

When we came up for air, I said, *"Man!"*

Jake brushed his knuckles against my cheek. "How long have you been up?"

"Now there's a leading question."

His mouth twitched, but he corrected, "Awake."

I squinted at the radio clock. "About forty-five minutes. The game's afoot, Watson."

"Oh, I'm Watson, am I?"

"Well..." I was hard pressed to be my usual witty self because Jake was tracing my bottom lip with his thumb, something I found distracting.

"How do you like being a detective now, Mr Holmes?"

Regretfully I shook my head.

"Scared?"

"You got that straight."

"Nice to know I got something straight." He kissed me again as I started to laugh. My mouth being open, he slipped his tongue in. I heard myself make some soft acquiescent sound. One of those blood-hot, dark-as-night kisses that usually leads to hot-blooded, dark-of-night acts – but did not this time.

Jake broke away and tumbled me off him, his hand grazing my ribs and bare back in final caress. I let the motion carry me, rolling off the bed on to my feet. Hunting for my shoes I pretended not to watch as Jake strode off to the bathroom, his heavy cock swinging free from the curling blond nest of his thighs.

Jake locked the door behind him; maybe he thought I might attack him in the shower.

I sat down to make a couple of phone calls.

First off I called Mr Gracen, my lawyer, and explained the situation at Spaniard's Hollow. In between the stunned silences, Mr Gracen cleared his throat and murmured, "I see." When I had finished outlining my adventures, he cleared his throat a final time and said, "Mr English, I shall have to consult my – ahem – associates. I shall have to consult the – ahem – penal and the health-and-welfare codes."

He promised to get back to me. I figured he intended to change his phone number the minute we said goodbye.

I called Angus but there was no answer at the shop. This was not a good sign. I needed to return to LA; Jake was right about that.

I tried the shop again, gave it up and phoned Lisa.

My mother was home prepping for one of her endless charity do's.

"Darling, why haven't you answered my calls? I've left simply dozens of messages with Andrew."

"Angus?"

"Angus, that's it. And Adrien, I know you don't like me to say so, but I do believe that boy is taking drugs."

I scowled at my reflection in the dark TV screen. "Lisa, I'm at the ranch."

"What ranch, darling? Oh, d'you mean that health farm I told you about?"

"What health – never mind. Lisa, I'm at the Pine Shadow."

She gave a little gasp. "*Why?* Why on earth would you want to go back to that dreadful place?"

"I'm writing. Lisa, I just wanted you to know –" I stopped. I wanted her to know where I was in case anything happened to me. After last night I knew that something *could* happen. But I couldn't tell Lisa that, so I said, "In case you need to get hold of me."

"Darling, I wish you wouldn't stay there. It's not very sanitary. And you know, the place is haunted."

"*Haunted?*"

"Oh you know that silly Indian legend about the monsters in the caves."

"What monsters in which caves?"

Lisa laughed her silvery laugh. "Don't tell me Mother Anna never told you? Now that I think of it, she probably made the whole thing up to frighten me. That woman always loathed me."

Jake came out of the bathroom, towelling his hair.

"What legend, Lisa?"

"Oh, heavens, darling. Every time a cow gets mutilated or a hiker disappears, people always claim it's UFOs or the Wolfen or whatever they called them."

"The Guardian?" Out of the corner of my eye I could see Jake shaking his head.

"Was that it?"

"Did Granna tell you that story, Lisa?"

"It may have been your father. He did like to tease." Lisa sighed, a sad, little heartfelt sound.

"But someone told you, right? It's a real legend?"

"A real legend? What does that mean, darling? Once upon a time someone told me a story. Your dreadful grandmama, I believe. It doesn't make it *true*."

She has her moments, does me mum.

When I put the receiver down at last I said to Jake, "Melissa didn't make up the story about The Devouring. There really is such a legend."

Jake had already caught the gist of my phone conversation. He retrieved his gun from under the bed pillow, saying, "Ghosts did not open fire on us last night, Adrien."

"I know that, but it proves Melissa is telling the truth."

"Which means zipola. So what if she didn't make up the story about The Devouring? Say she does believe it. Say she believes it with all her heart and feels obliged to act it out."

"What about the dog?"

"What dog?"

"Kevin's dog. Marquez confirmed the story that the dog was torn to pieces."

"Apples and oranges. A dog is killed by coyotes. That has nothing to do with someone shooting at us. Or with murdering Livingston – if he is – was – the stiff in the barn."

"It might have."

Jake put his hands on his hips. "Are you going to sit there and tell me you believe Livingston was killed by ancient Indian spirits using rifles?"

"Of course not."

"Coyotes using rifles?"

"Come on, Jake."

"No, you come on, Adrien." He unlocked the chain and opened the hotel room door. "Come on," he repeated.

"Where are we going?"

"We're going to eat breakfast and then we're going to file a report with the sheriff."

*

Leaving Jake at Granny Parker's Pantry, I darted across the street to get my own prescription filled on the pretext of filling his. No harm in providing a little backup for the happy, positive thoughts, but the last thing I wanted was Jake thinking I was a liability.

A few minutes later, watching Jake perform his own version of The Devouring I said, "If someone is up to something at the site, Professor Shoup gets my vote."

"Why's that?"

I told him Mel's story. Jake listened and at last said, "Mel Davis. Why's that name familiar?"

"I doubt if he has a record."

Jake looked unconvinced. At last he said, "Davis. Wasn't he the guy you were shacked up with?"

When I was suspected of being a serial killer Jake had investigated my background with the attention usually reserved for Supreme Court nominees by opposing political parties.

I said, "How romantic you make that sound."

"You stayed friends."

"Sure. Why not?"

Jake went back to shovelling through his eggs and bacon. He said finally, "So what happened?"

"Mel didn't know. The university may have released Shoup or he may have left on his own."

"No. Between you and Davis."

Good question. I wasn't sure I knew myself. Despite Mel's protests, I always believed it had to do with his fear that he might get saddled with an invalid one day. I set down my orange juice and said colourlessly, "We went in different directions, that's all."

Jake snorted. "Yeah, about four hundred miles."

When the feeding frenzy was over, we repaired to the sheriff-sub-station where I let Jake do the jawing. My popularity rating had not exactly soared since the snake-o-gram, and we all politely pretended I was not present. Jake gave the cops a brief, accurate account of the shooting the night before which we signed in triplicate.

I studied the wanted posters on the bulletin board above a bank of dented filing cabinets while Jake asked whether they'd had any luck identifying the DB in the County Morgue.

No. They had not.

Jake inquired whether they'd had anyone in from the archeologist's camp in Spaniard's Hollow to try and make an ID?

A little ripple of unease ran through the assembly as Sheriff Billingsly bristled. "What are you getting at, Detective?"

"Just an idea," Jake said off-handedly.

It was one that had not occurred to anyone else, and they seemed disinclined to discuss it.

Then Jake asked about the bullet that had killed John Doe. I thought for sure they would show him the door but they did not. After a moment Billingsly tossed a file across the desk. Jake told me later the report read that John Doe had been killed by a .22 calibre hollowpoint. He had been dead at least ten days.

As we started for the glass doors, Jake asked in apparent afterthought, "Any word on Ted Harvey?"

No word on Harvey.

When we got back to the ranch, Jake insisted on swabbing down the Bronco. As I watched the soapy water in the bucket turn pink, I started to feel queasy, and as Jake seemed disinclined to discuss 'the case,' I retreated to the house. Firing up the laptop, I re-read my half-hearted efforts of the past few days.

It didn't help that my characters were as unlikable as the originals in *Titus Andronicus*. Even my protagonist Jason was beginning to bug me. I was trying to decide if I could possibly kill him off in the middle of the book when Jake came in to inform me he was going to hunt for shell casings.

"Don't trip over the Sheriff's Department," I warned him, dragging my attention from my magnum dopus.

"I won't." He hesitated. "Hey, don't go wandering off, okay?"

"Like where?"

"Like anywhere."

"Oh." I weighed this nugget. "You mean you think someone might try to..."

Duh.

"Roger, will co," I said and sketched him a salute.

Jake shook his head like it was hopeless, and left me to the murderous intrigue of the Andronici family.

I typed recklessly for an hour, refuelled on coffee and hit the book again.

The sound of a truck in the front yard startled me out of my beta rhythm. Muttering rude things, I padded out on to the porch. Kevin was swinging down from his green truck. Briefly it went through my mind that if Kevin were a bad guy, now would be the time to make his move.

It also occurred to me that having a truck that could pass, from a distance, as a forest ranger's vehicle could be a handy way of getting around unseen at night.

"All hell's breaking loose," Kevin informed me as he reached the porch stairs. His youthful face appeared older and strained.

"Let me guess. More ghostly chanting from the caves last night?"

Kevin looked puzzled. "No, but some bastard dumped our tools in the lake. Every shovel, pick, axe, you name it. We've been fishing equipment out all morning. The water's like ice this time of year."

"Don't you keep watch at night?"

"Sure, but no one saw anything."

"A likely story. Who was the sentry last night?"

"Melissa took first watch. A guy named Bob Grainger took the second."

To give myself time, I offered Kevin a chair and asked if he'd like a beer. He accepted the chair, declined the drink, and then changed his mind. I brought him a beer and he took it from me, announcing, "They found Dr Livingston."

I didn't quite know what to say. Kevin was staring at me expectantly.

"They found his car parked in town. It's been sitting in the parking lot of some hotel. No one noticed."

Did that mean Livingston had been killed in town? Or had his killer driven the site supervisor's car into Basking and then hitched a ride back? Pretty damn risky. Not as risky as killing Livingston in town and then transporting his body back to the ranch though.

Maybe the killer had had an accomplice?

If Livingston had been killed at the site and his car moved, there had to be a reason for it. The most likely reason I could think of was that it was important to someone that it appear Livingston had left on his trip as planned. Someone was buying time.

In the face of my silence Kevin burst out, "They've confiscated all our guns. Amy's .45, Livingston's Rugar and my rifle. They think one of *us* might have shot him."

"Why?"

Kevin shook his head. "I couldn't believe it at first, but now..."

"Now what?"

"Well, somebody shot him. I guess – I mean –" He gave me a funny look. "You didn't ask where they found him. You already know, don't you?" His tone was accusing.

I admitted awkwardly, "That Livingston's was the body we found in the barn? We sort of – Jake sort of put two and two together."

"Why would someone hide him in *your* barn? That's what we're all asking ourselves."

Among other things, I bet.

I said, "There's a good chance he wouldn't have been found for a long time. It seems like Harvey didn't go in the barn much."

"Harvey has to be the one who killed him."

I didn't say anything, but I was thinking, *then who killed Harvey?*

Kevin drank his beer and then said, "It doesn't make sense. None of this makes sense. And another thing: there were a couple of nights when my truck was taken without my knowing. Probably someone just borrowed it, but what if – what if – ?"

"For what reason?" I asked neutrally.

"None. There is none."

"Think about it. There has to be some reason. When was your truck taken?"

"I don't remember for sure. Last week. Maybe Thursday."

Thursday night was the night Harvey had been killed.

My expression must have been odd, because Kevin rushed on, "Livingston was shot with a .22 hollow point. My rifle is loaded with .22 hollow points." He shook his head, looking sick and scared. "A long-rifle cartridge is a hunting round, you know? It's not like I'm the only guy around here with a .22 calibre." He put his head in his hands. "Adrien, what am I going to do?"

I was afraid he was going to cry. I shifted over next to him on the sofa and put my arm around his shoulders. It was the big brother brand of hug, mind you.

But then Kevin wrapped his arms around me, and his mood

seemed less fraternal than mine.

"Er... Kevin," I began, trying to pry him loose.

And then with the timing of a French farce, Jake opened the door. He stood stock-still. I could hear the clock ticking on the mantel. I hadn't heard him drive up. I hadn't heard the front door. And I hadn't, off the top of my head, anything to say.

Jake did though. Right on cue he drawled, "Meanwhile, back at the ranch..."

Eleven

"Kevin was just leaving," I said, managing to detach myself from Kevin.

"Did he mistake you for the door?"

"It's not what you think," Kevin chimed in. Not really a helpful remark.

Jake said, still cool but suddenly dangerous, "How would you know what I think?"

Now that I had Kevin on his feet, I steered him towards the doorway. He and Jake sidled past each other like tomcats from rival gangs. Jake was wearing the sort of sneer that begs someone to take a swipe at it.

"Does that asshole bully you?" Kevin demanded as I slid him across the polished floor.

"You're kidding, right?" I handed Kevin his jacket and thrust him out on to the porch. "We'll talk," I hissed, and closed the door in his face.

"Kevin's worried about being arrested," I informed Jake, finding him in the kitchen chugalugging from a milk carton (something I hate).

Jake slam-dunked the empty carton into the trash bin with what I'd call a controlled use of force.

I rattled on to fill the silence, "The body in our barn was Livingston's. The cops are checking everyone's guns at the site for a ballistics match. Livingston was shot with a .22 calibre, and Kevin owns a .22."

"Maybe Kevin shot him."

I shook my head.

"I see, Mr Pinkerton. And you base this deduction on the fact the kid has a nice ass and a freckled nose?"

"I base it on the fact that I don't think he did it. What motive would he have?"

"Maybe he didn't like the guy. Maybe Livingston was failing him in class or kicking him off the dig. Maybe the good doctor found out the kid was buying and selling pot from Ted Harvey. Maybe the professor tried to put a move on the kid; sexual favours for GPA points. It wouldn't be the first time in the history of the world."

I felt my jaw drop. "Where are you getting this from?"

"Hey," said Jake, "I'm just throwing out possibilities. One thing about a homicide investigation: you can always find a motive. If the rest of the case fits – opportunity, means – go with it. The motive will show eventually."

I chewed this over. Jake was the expert here, but I didn't peg Kevin for a killer. Not that I was dumb enough to say so.

I shrugged. "Maybe. I've got an idea or two of my own."

"I knew that was coming."

"But I need your help."

Jake raised his eyes as though seeking divine intervention. "Hell, I live to serve," he assured me, closing the fridge door with a little bang.

No doubt he was waxing sarcastic, but two hours later there we were, Mr Pinkerton and Inspector Bull hot on the trail. Well, actually off the trail and on the cliff overlooking Spaniard's Hollow.

"That's about a two-hundred-foot drop," Jake was saying, evidently triangulating in his head like a well-trained Eagle Scout. His nose was pink with cold and allergies. He wiped it on his sleeve.

"It's pretty steep," I agreed, squinting down at a dizzying panorama of treetops, grass, and the tarn shining like a mirror in the late afternoon sun. "There must be a path."

Keeping hold of the branch of a scrub oak, which grew over the drop at a gravity-defying angle, I leaned further out. Pebbles shifted under my boots and bounced down the mountainside, clacking off boulders.

"Watch it, for Chrissake!" Jake's fist fastened in my collar and hair, dragging me back. I landed sprawled in his lap – which in other circumstances I might have relished.

"Easy! Take it easy." I freed myself, yanking my shirt collar back into place. "I know what I'm doing."

"My mistake, Sir Edmund Hilary." Jake took my place at the edge and cautiously peered down. "There's no path."

"Well maybe not a path as you and I would recognise the word."

The edge, apparently only held together by the tree roots and tiny wildflowers, began to crumble beneath Jake. I yelled a warning.

Jake did a kind of reverse salamander as I grabbed for his legs and hauled, lying all the way back in the grass and pine needles. His boot heel grazed my jaw as he kicked around trying to save himself, and I had to let go of his shins.

With amazing agility in one so large, Jake rolled over and snapped into a crouch like a kung fu fighter.

"This is a lousy idea!" he snarled. His face had a *mal-de-mer*ish tinge.

"Are you afraid of heights?"

"No!"

Uh huh.

I thought it over, chewing the inside of my cheek. "I can do it."

His mouth worked but nothing came out. "You are fucking *nuts*," he managed at last, glaring at me.

"I'm also about fifty pounds lighter than you."

"What does that have to do with it? You can't fly. Not to mention you've got a bad heart."

I wished he hadn't brought that up because despite the stress and strain of the past week I was feeling healthier and stronger than I had in years. Maybe it was all that fresh air and exercise. Or maybe I was kidding myself. Whatever, I didn't want Jake thinking I was less of a man than he was.

"Forget about my heart. We can tie the rope to that tree." I pointed to a sturdy looking pine. "If it comes down to it, you can pull me up a hell of a lot more easily than I could pull you up."

"No." He shook his head. "No way, Adrien. Absolutely not."

"I can do this, Jake. Don't – I don't have trouble with normal physical exertion."

"Scaling cliffs is not normal physical exertion!"

"I'm not planning to climb up. I'll follow the trail to the bottom." The more he argued against it, the more important it was to me to do it. I urged, "Come *on*, Jake, we're going to lose the light."

Jake wasn't budging.

I cajoled, "I'm just going to walk down this little trail. I'm not a – Jake, you spent how the hell many hours hunting for tyre tracks and spent bullets and shell casings? And we've got *nada* to show for it."

Temper turned his eyes almost yellow. "So we start exploring Indian caves? Adrien, no secret Indian sect is hunting us. No ghostly Kuksu shot at us last night."

"You can't say that these things are unconnected. Kevin said that only last night someone dumped all the shovels and tools at the site into the lake."

Jake raked a hand through his crisp hair in a barely restrained movement. "Listen to yourself."

"It would be nice if someone would! I'm not saying I expect to find a ghostly assassin lurking in the cave. Although, you know, no one has ever seen a subconscious, yet scientists believe in the subconscious. No one has seen the Id, but Freud and plenty of psychiatrists believe in the Id. Why is it so hard –"

"I don't believe in ghosts," Jake interrupted. "I don't believe in extra-terrestrials. You can find people who do believe in these things, you probably believe in these things."

"Do you believe in God?"

"God is different."

"Why is God different? Nobody has ever seen him. Her. It."

Jake yelled, "I'm not going to sit on a mountain top arguing theology, psychology, what-the-hell-ology with you! I don't think we have probable cause to risk our necks exploring this cave."

"I disagree."

"Then you can risk *your* neck."

I shrugged and turned back to the cliff edge. Jake grabbed my arm.

"Just wait a goddamn minute." His fingers dug in.

"Ow...what for?"

"You can't do this on your own!"

"Watch me." I tried to stare him down.

Jake held my gaze for a long moment and then his mouth twitched. He gave my arm a little shake and then released me. "You're supposed to give up now."

"We're wasting daylight."

"Shit!" Swearing under his breath, Jake tossed me one end of the line we had lugged up the mountain, and fastened the other end around the stalwart-looking pine.

I knotted my end around my waist.

"This is a bad idea," Jake growled.

"You said that."

His scowl was my parting gift as I stepped carefully over the edge.

The rope was only a precaution; I figured I could find a way down the slope finding footholds among the rocks, and hanging on to the branches and wayward roots of hardy shrubs. But the first thing I discovered was that the incline was sharper than it looked; more suitable for repelling than strolling. Leech-like I clung to the mountainside and considered Plan B.

Sweat prickled along my hairline, trickled between my shoulder blades and dried in the crisp forest air.

A rock gave beneath my boot heel and I dropped down. It was only a few inches, maybe a foot, but my heart didn't seem to travel with the rest of my body, and for a few seconds I had a scared taste of what it would feel like to really fall. The rope scraped painfully over my ribs, nipples, and caught under my underarms.

I kicked around till my foot found a place to lodge; my clawing fingers dug in, and I was steady once again with the entrance of the cave just below me.

I lifted up my eyes. Jake was about fifty feet above, still lowering. I gave him the thumbs up. If he responded I couldn't tell. Untying the rope, I jumped down to the cave ledge, landing in an awkward crouch. Picking myself up, I stood, brushing my hands off on my Levi's.

There was a yellow jacket nest right outside the cave; bees

buzzed around my head in angry bullets.

Ducking a couple of dive-bombers, I switched on my flashlight, turning towards the heart of darkness. A mere few footsteps in, I realised I needed a stronger flashlight.

The feeble beam played over the walls. Faintly, I could make out paintings, figures scrawled in rusty brown like dried blood: wavy lines and circles and something that could easily be spacemen. Nothing conclusive, mind you, no little stick figures with fangs.

I walked further into the cave. It tunnelled deeply into the hillside. Instead of the expected shallow recess, I had found a real cavern.

I started as a yellow jacket buzzed by my ear.

Follow the bouncing ball, I thought as the white circle of the flashlight beam danced along. Several yards in, my flashlight picked out a small skeleton. I stopped, nudging it with my foot. Too big for a rabbit, too small for a dog. A fox?

"Feet start moving," I said under my breath, and was startled when my whisper came back to me in an eerie echo.

I went on for what felt like a mile or two.

The cave was as cold as a cellar, and it stank with the decay of animal nests and animal droppings. I began to wonder why it had been so important to me to make this trek. The darkness seemed to press in from all sides.

After another dozen yards I decided that I had gone far enough; that there was no need to track the cave all the way to the end. I was losing my nerve, no doubt about it, and I wasn't quite sure why. I tried to distract myself by analysing it. It didn't help.

Though I've never been claustrophobic, I began to feel trapped. The darkness was heavy, smothering.

I told myself to get a grip.

One more reluctant footstep. Then another shuffle forward.

And right as I decided to call it quits, psych or no psych, the flashlight ray lit on something that at first glance I took to be a log. I stopped dead. It was not a log. It was a body, filthy, covered with yellow jackets and insects.

I started backing up, stepped on something round and hard, and lost my balance. I hit the floor of the cave, and the light went out.

Frantically I groped for the flashlight. My fingers closed on something round, not quite smooth, which crumbled in my hand. I knew what that had to be, and I did yell then, tossing it away.

More fumbling before I found the flashlight again. I shook it hard into life, my near-hysterical relief disproportionate to that watery light – which picked out the pieces of a small animal skull.

Scrambling up, I bolted for the mouth of the cave.

My feet pounded the hard-packed dirt as I ran, chasing the little white moon of my flashlight beam.

It seemed to take a long time to find the entrance. Too long. I stopped and tried to calm myself down as the darkness closed in. That's all it was: darkness. An absence of light. But it seemed to stand beside me like a hostile physical presence. Beside me and all around me; looming, menacing…

There were no branch tunnels. There was only the one way; so I was either running towards the opening or I was running deeper into the cave.

My pulse skipped a beat. Had I got turned around somehow? Was I running deeper into the bowels of the mountain? Why wasn't it getting lighter?

I stood there, huffing and puffing, my heart shaking with fright. *No damn way*, I argued against my rising panic. *No damn way did I lose my bearings so much that I ran further into this cave.*

When I had myself back under control, I resumed walking, but slowly, fighting the conviction that with each step I was moving further from safety. Commonsense told me to keep going, to trust my instincts.

The longest journey begins with the first step, so the philosophers say, and so I said to myself over and over. Me and the Energizer Bunny, I thought. We keep going and going and going...

To my everlasting relief I saw that the blackness was thinning, giving way to milky gloom. I had been deceived by the simple fact that daylight was fading. It was dusk.

Reaching the cave entrance, I ducked back as something stung my hand. A yellow jacket. I swore, sucked the back of my hand, and reconnoitred.

Unless the dead man had been killed in the cave, there had to be a trail leading up from the glen below. No one could have lugged that dead weight up a cliff. Working from this premise made it easier. The path was there, I just had to find it. I sat on my haunches, catching my breath and scanning the pine-studded mountainside. Finally I spotted a dirt path trickling down through the trees.

"Jake!"

At my shout Jake leaned out over the edge once more. I gestured that I was heading on down, not coming back up. He made some kind of complicated hand gestures and withdrew.

I started down the path, taking it as quickly as I could without breaking my neck. It took about twenty minutes. Loose rocks and pine needles slowed my progress, and required my full attention. If I'd been carrying a dead weight uphill it would have taken even longer.

At long last I found myself on terra firma. This was an improvement but not as much as I had hoped. The surrounding trees effectively blocked the remaining light. It was very quiet. Too quiet? There's nothing like finding a decayed body to throw the old radar out of whack. Reassuringly, a cricket chirped.

Shaking off the jitters, I got moving. I knew it would take Jake at least half an hour to get back to the ranch, grab one of the vehicles and drive around to pick me up. Half an hour in Creepsville would be plenty. I booked.

It grew darker. I trudged on. The birds in the trees stopped sympathizing and fell silent. I heard a crack behind me like a twig snapping under foot.

I stopped. Tried to figure out where the noise came from.

The sound came again, closer. And with it came a scent I can't quite describe. A musky odor, heavy and oily, animal.

It was hard for me to pinpoint my location since I was not familiar with this part of the woods. I took a moment to locate Saddleback Mountain and make sure I was heading east, towards the archeologist's camp.

I paced myself, not wanting to risk a sprain on the uneven track, and hoping I wasn't over-taxing my strength. I didn't seem to have a choice.

Whatever followed me, moving through the bushes, could be heard plainly now. And I knew that if it was an animal, a bear or a big cat, running was liable to trigger an attack. Not that I believed there was a bear or a mountain lion stalking me, but it was not impossible. Reason told me to walk; I picked up speed, breaking into a lope.

My muscles burned, sweat soaking my shirt. I started worrying about pushing myself too hard. Kind of a drag if the last words I heard on earth were Jake's 'I told you so.'

Surely the camp couldn't be much further? Up ahead I spotted the markers that staked out the location of the Red Rover mine. Maybe another mile? I ran faster, listening to the scared but steady thump of blood in my ears.

Jogging around a bend, I nearly got creamed by Jake, who was tearing up the road in the Bronco.

I jumped left, Jake swerved right and braked.

I rolled out of the bank of leaves, picked myself up and clambered into the Bronco.

"For Chrissake, Adrien!" He swiped off the reflective sunglasses.

"There's something out there!" I gasped, double-checking that I had locked the door. My heart was going like a trip-hammer. I shut up and listened to its beat.

Jake's face fell into hard dangerous lines. Pulling his gun out of his shoulder holster, he reached for the door handle.

I grabbed for him. "What are you doing?"

"What do you think is out there?"

"I don't know. An animal?"

I must not have sounded convincing. "That's what I thought." He gave me a long, level look. "Wait here." Shaking my hand off, he climbed out.

He just didn't get it.

I climbed out too, none too happy about it, watching tensely as Jake strode back up the road. He looked ready for trouble, though he clearly believed I was a victim of my own imagination. I trailed behind, wanting to keep the jeep in sprinting distance, but not wanting to lose sight of Jake.

While we waited my heart slowed back down to a regular tempo. I relaxed a bit. Felt even a little triumphant. I had done what I had set out to do and I was none the worse for it.

A few yards ahead of me Jake stood still. I stopped in my tracks. Nothing moved in the twilight. Not a twig stirred, not a blade of grass bent. Beyond the sound of the jeep engine running quietly down the road, there was utter and unnerving silence.

I could hardly make out Jake in the gloaming.

"It's gone," I called.

Jake shook his head.

He was right. I could feel it too; something *was* there, beyond our line of vision, listening to us as we listened for it.

I can't explain it, but suddenly I was about as scared as I've ever been in my life. More scared even than the night before when people had been shooting at us.

"Jake –" I broke off as a long, blood-curdling howl broke the stillness.

It was not a coyote. I've heard enough coyotes to tell the difference. It sounded like... well... a wolf. Close by.

Jake brought his gun up into a firing stance, but the echo didn't seem to come from any one direction.

"Jesus," he said just loudly enough for me to hear him.

Without conscious decision, I started back for the jeep. I meant to walk but somehow I found myself going hell-for-leather.

Jake was right behind me, slamming and locking his door a half-minute after me.

"I'm not imagining it," I said.

"No."

He shifted into reverse, resting his arm on the back of my seat as he turned to guide our backwards retreat.

I stared at what I could see of his face in the gloom. "You felt it too."

I knew it wasn't logical, rational or even plausible, that nameless dread, but we were running from it. *Jake* was running from it.

We reached a point in the road where there was space for Jake to turn the jeep around, which he did with a smooth efficiency that belied the fact his hands weren't quite steady yet.

"I found something," I said abruptly, remembering the cave. (Proof of what we had just experienced, the corpse in the cave was an afterthought.) "Not what I expected. I found a body. In the cave."

Jake spared me half a glance. "Not what you expected? What did you expect?" His blond brows drew together. "Was it...?"

I knew what – and why – he asked.

"I think so." Belatedly queasy, I said, "Animals have been at it."

We got to the ranch and Jake called it in while I poured us each a drink. When Jake got off the phone I said, "We don't have to go back up there, do we?"

"I'll go. You can stay here."

I wasn't crazy about that idea either.

We drank our bourbon in silence.

"This is nuts," I said at last.

Jake swished his bourbon through his teeth and swallowed, making a kind of "Ahhh..."

I was very tired and the bourbon was hitting me hard, spreading a melting drowsiness through my veins. I heard my voice slur a little as I asked, "Why would anyone kill Ted Harvey *and* Dr Livingston? What could they possibly have in common?"

"If it is Harvey," Jake replied.

"Okay, if it is, why?"

"Maybe one of them was killed by mistake."

"Why do you say that?"

"You thought they looked alike, right?"

"No. I knew Livingston wasn't Harvey. Everyone else thought my description of Harvey fit Livingston. I didn't."

Jake shrugged as though this proved his point.

"These two have nothing in common. One is a respected academic. The other is well, kind of a low life."

"They've got something in common. Presumably the same

person killed them. Presumably that person had a motive."

I swiveled my glass on the table, clockwise, counter-clockwise. "You think it's Kevin."

Jake shrugged. "Suppose Harvey and the kid have a business arrangement. Suppose Livingston finds out about it. The kid kills the professor. He falls out with Harvey, and kills Harvey."

Jake's tour of duty as a cop tended to colour his worldview as through a glass darkly.

I blinked at him. My eyelids felt weighted, "Jake, there's no reason to suspect Kevin more than anyone else."

"How about a .22 calibre rifle?"

"We don't even know if ballistics got a match."

"I think they will get a match, Adrien." His eyes met mine. "I know you like the kid, but there's usually not a lot of mystery about these things. You gather the facts and you put them together, and they usually add up to one person, even if there's not always enough evidence for a conviction."

I didn't get a chance to argue this (even if I'd had an argument), because the sheriffs showed up, and Jake left to show them the cave. As for me, I'd had about all I could take for one day. I sacked out on my bed for a couple of hours of deep dreamless sleep. When I woke I felt like the new and improved model and I treated myself to a long soak in the claw-foot hot tub, doctored up my yellow jacket bite, which was now an unattractive red welt, pulled on a pair of sweats and a soft T-shirt, and started dinner.

While the pork chops broiled, I sat down at the table with a legal pad and tried to make sense of what Jake and I had learned so far.

The truth, the whole truth and nothing but the truth, I told myself. But what was the truth?

One – Someone was willing to kill me and/or Jake.

Why? It's not like I was such a threat as an amateur sleuth. Was there another motive for wanting to get rid of me and/or Jake?

Two – Someone had killed two men. Two men who, on the surface, had nothing in common – except maybe they looked alike to someone.

So maybe they did have something in common? Or maybe killing one had been an accident? Or maybe the same person hadn't killed both men?

Three – Someone (I refused to think some*thing*) was harassing the archeologists at Spanish Hollow.

Why? Because someone held that ground to be sacred? Or because someone *wanted* to bring attention to the dig?

I thought about what Marquez had said about Shoup wanting a 'big discovery.' That meant publicity, right? Mysterious goings-on at a site could generate a certain amount of publicity.

Did these three things add up? I had another whisky and considered them.

The snake incident had happened after I let it spill that Jake was a cop, so maybe his being a cop figured in?

Except, as Melissa pointed out, there were few secrets in a small town. Billingsly knew Jake was a cop. The word could have spread before I ever opened my big mouth. Marnie Starr knew Jake was a cop.

Which meant?

The snake could have been intended for me, but Jake was the one who had been shot. And now that I thought about it, one of the pictures I'd seen at Marnie's had been of Marnie holding a rifle like she meant business.

Maybe Harvey's death was unconnected to Livingston's after all? Or maybe Marnie knew Livingston, too? I tapped the pen on the yellow pad, studying the myriad random dots as though I could connect them in a meaningful pattern.

Reluctantly I considered what had happened in the hollow this afternoon. Something *had* happened. But what? A strange animal smell, a feeling of being watched, a hair-raising howl that *could* have been a dog or a coyote: these things were hardly evidence.

In fact, I would have blamed my panicked reaction on too much imagination, except that Jake had experienced – and reacted – to it.

It? Group hysteria maybe? Was Jake more suggestible than he seemed? More... sensitive?

I doubted it.

We had experienced something today, but how did it relate? *Did* it relate? Could the occurrences at the camp not be man-made? Even I had trouble swallowing that one.

It was several hours before Jake returned, looking weary and grim.

"Was it Harvey?" I asked watching him scrub up at the sink.

"Yeah, they're ninety percent sure it is."

"Was he shot?"

"Yeah."

I trailed Jake to the front room, watching as he poured himself a stiff drink.

"Do you think it was the same weapon?"

"Adrien, get real." Jake downed his drink in a gulp and poured another.

I understood why he might be feeling a little tense. "I simply mean, was there anything to indicate it wasn't the same weapon?"

Jake drifted into the kitchen as he answered, "It's not like I had – or wanted – a chance to examine the wounds." He opened the oven broiler. "Mm. Charcoal briquettes. My favourite."

"They're a little dried out. I didn't know how long you'd be."

Jake gave me a deadpan look.

"Why don't you have a shower," I suggested. "Take it from me, you'll feel better. I'll fix you a plate." He handed his glass to me. "And another drink."

A shower and another drink put Jake in a more agreeable mood – or maybe my having another drink made it seem so. Anyway, over his withered chops and mushy vegetables he described for me how they had climbed down to the cave and retrieved Harvey's body, carrying it down by stretcher which, at night, must have been pretty grim.

"Are they going to arrest Kevin?"

He didn't meet my eyes. "Adrien, I'm not in their confidence."

"Would you arrest Kevin if this was your case?"

He shrugged. "There are a lot of factors involved in timing an arrest. At this point, I'd want a tighter case. Something to take to court."

"Do you think I'm still considered a suspect?"

He pushed his plate away. Now his eyes did meet mine. "You're suspect all right. I just don't know that it's murder they suspect you of."

I considered this.

"Jake, you know what happened in the woods today –"

"Here we go," he muttered. "*The Blair Witch Project.*"

"Hey, you were there."

"These men were shot to death. The Guardian did not rip them to pieces like that dog – not that the dog was ripped to pieces by supernatural beings. The Guardian is a legend. A folk tale. It's not – I admit there was something funky about the woods today, okay? But I'm not prepared to – I mean –" He shook his head, denying all and any paranormal possibilities.

Not that I blamed him. For all that I prided myself on keeping an open mind, I wasn't ready to log into the Supernatural Zone.

I redeemed myself from the pork chop fiasco by coming up with Jake's favourite raspberry and dark chocolate Portofino ice cream for dessert. There's nothing like a pint of ice cream to soothe the savage beast. Or possibly it was the alcohol. Jake could sure put it away, but that was typical of cops, according to Jake.

Catching my speculative gaze, Jake's mouth twisted. "You've had too much to drink."

"*I* have?"

He nodded. "I can always tell. You start giving me these looks." He propped his chin on his hand and dropped his eyelids to half-mast, imitating me I suppose. I have to admit it was a pretty sappy expression.

"Come hither," he stated.

"Pardon?"

"That's your come-hither look."

Reluctantly I laughed. "And this is my go-to-hell look."

He sighed, a regretful sound like blowing into a beer bottle. "You are probably the best-looking guy I ever knew."

"A bottle of whisky helps."

"No, seriously. You are... Your eyes and everything. Not my type, but beautiful."

"What is your type?"

"A girl."

"Bullshit."

His head jerked up and he gave me a bright hostile look.

"Bullshit," I said again. Maybe I *had* had too much to drink because I wasn't backing off, although I saw it go through Jake's soggy brain to pop me one.

Instead Jake said clearly and coldly, "I've got nothing to offer you, Adrien." These were not the opening remarks to a proposal.

"I don't recall asking." For good measure, I added, "Hell, you came after me, Jake. Every step of the way."

I don't know how we jumped from mild flirtation to open hostility. A few too many drinks, I guess. I figured Jake's next move would be to stomp out the door. I didn't want him to walk away, but I knew I couldn't stand down. Not about this.

Jake eyeballed me for a long moment then he shrugged. The tension was gone, just like that. He refilled his glass, held it up briefly in a salute and knocked it back.

"So," he said casually, "You want to fuck?"

Twelve

"Sure," I said.

But I was less sure when we walked into my bedroom and undressed. For one thing, I knew sex wasn't going to solve anything, but it might change things. For the worse.

Secondly, as I watched Jake unbuckle his belt in a business-like fashion, I remembered that this was a guy who liked to do it with whips and chains – and strangers.

If we could have fallen to the kitchen floor, swept away on a tide of passion… but the lag time of walking to the bedroom, stripping, lying down on the bed… it gave time to think. To reflect. To pause.

Jake knelt on the bed and slipped his condom on with a little snap like a detective donning latex gloves to examine a crime scene. Not a romantic noise.

I'd had enough to drink that I should have been incapable of rational thought, but for some damn reason, I was still thinking. I felt a little detached, a little distant as Jake bent over me.

The muscles on his arms stood out like ropes, his big hands denting the mattress on either side of me as he balanced himself. His cock looked like a warhead; I felt my eyes going wide. I had waited a long time for this moment though this wasn't exactly the moment I had waited for. Suddenly there seemed to be knees and elbows everywhere.

"Ouch," Jake said.

"Sorry."

He bent forward at the same moment I raised my head, and we banged noses.

"What the hell?" Jake's voice came out muffledly behind his hand.

"Sorry."

"You've done this before, right?"

I don't know why that hit me as funny, but I started to laugh, and Jake pushed back and said exasperatedly, "What the hell is so funny?"

I shook my head.

"You sure know how to break the mood." However he didn't appear to be giving up. His mouth found mine and he kissed me.

Whoopee ty yi yea!

Suddenly it was going to be okay. Better than okay.

I kissed Jake back, tasting the licorice-bite of the whisky on his tongue. He licked my mouth, which was different, sort of playful. My lips parted, anticipating, but he softly bit the side of my neck – and then a little harder. There was a lot of strength and heat in the body poised over mine. He smelled good, like my almond soap, and he tasted good, and he felt very good, his hand between my thighs doing things other men had done, but in his own way.

We realigned ourselves, the mattress squeaking noisily, and I raised my legs over Jake's shoulders. I wasn't expecting much in the way of foreplay, and I didn't get it. Jake pressed into me and I gritted my jaw as my muscles submitted.

"You with me?"

I grunted acknowledgment. Oh yeah, I was with him.

He began to rock against me, and I hung on for the ride of my life: a day at the rodeo and the Fourth of July all rolled into one. Yeeha!

*

"Christ, you're limber."

He'd had plenty of opportunity to find it out last night. I turned my head. Jake stood in the doorway of the front room observing me going through my bi-monthly routine.

"Tai Chi," I informed him, palms resting on the floor.

"Looks more like ballet."

"I took ballet. This is Tai Chi."

"You took ballet?" Jake sounded horrified. He stopped scratching his sun-browned belly. "Your mother is an example of why people should have to have a licence to have kids."

I straightened up. "Lay off my mother."

"Ballet but not the Boy Scouts? It's your mother's fault you're queer."

I exhaled fast, serenity vanishing in a puff of morning breath.

"Listen, asshole – and I use the term deliberately – my mother is not the reason I'm queer. If she'd opted for the Boy Scouts or military school I'd just be a different kind of queer, okay? Secondly, I don't know that 'fault' is the right word. This is how God made me. You are how God made you. All God's little chillun are how God made 'em. You think God made a mistake, take it up with Him."

I scrubbed my face with my towel, threw it at Jake and stalked off to the shower.

By the time I was bathed and groomed and feeling like my normal mild-mannered self, Jake had breakfast on the table. I don't know if this was a peace offering or if he simply didn't trust my cooking after the night before.

"French toast?" I said doubtfully.

"The breakfast of champions. You want jam or shall I melt

brown sugar for syrup?"

That sounded fairly ghastly. I said, "Maybe just coffee?"

My much-maligned mater couldn't have looked more disapproving. I got my coffee with a plate of French toast spread thickly with crab-apple jelly, and Jake sat down across from me, elbows propped on the table. He applied himself to his vittles as though someone were paying him time and a half to finish ahead of schedule.

I said, "I thought I'd do some research in town this morning."

He nodded, not glancing up from his plate. "Watch your back."

Now that struck me as a little too disinterested. I speculated on what Jake's plans might be?

"Eat your breakfast," he grunted.

I washed the sweet toast down with a mouthful of hot coffee while I reconsidered. Maybe he was trying to ditch me, but these days the majority of detective work is done by computer. Let Jake try his way, and I'd try mine. And may the best man win.

I checked first with the town newspaper. Back in the glory days, *The Basking Express* had been called *The Basking Gazette*. The first issue had been printed in 1887.

There was a newspaper morgue, but it only went back ten years. Everything earlier had been shipped to the library where it had been copied on microfilm.

That was the story at *The Basking Express* anyway. The library had a different story.

"We never got the funding," Miss Buttermit, the rhinestone librarian informed me.

"So nothing is on microfilm?"

"Oh, it's not so bad as that. We were able to copy the newspapers back to circa the 1920's."

"What happened to the newspapers before circa the 1920s?"

Miss Buttermit's pale eyes flickered behind the kitschy glasses. "They've been preserved. To an extent."

"To what extent?"

"To the extent that they are bound in hardcover in the basement."

I asked tentatively, "Would it be possible to – ?"

"Only library personnel have access to the basement," she regretted firmly.

I thought this over.

"What was it you were looking for, Mr English?"

That was the crux of it. I did not have a theory; I did not really even have a hypothesis. Basically I had a hunch.

Handing Miss B some meaningless response, I headed for the computers, and spent the morning pouring over microfilmed copies of *The Basking Gazette*, getting the *Gazette's* spin on such world-shaping events as Vietnam, Gandhi's assassination and the completion of the Cascade Tunnel.

I read my great-grandfather's obituary, and the announcement of my grandmother's engagement to Thomas English. Rolls of 35mm later I read my grandmother's obit.

Interesting but not germane. If my hunch was right, the answer I was seeking was buried in the distant past, buried deep with the crumbling foundations of the early days of Basking Township.

I went out for a cup of coffee and returned to the library.

"Who do I have to talk to about getting access to the volumes in the basement?" I asked Miss Buttermit.

"You would have to call the head of Reference and make an appointment. We have to know why you want to examine those old and fragile research materials." Her faded eyes blinked suspiciously at me from behind the cat-eye shaped lenses.

I said, "I'm a writer. I'm researching a book."

She repeated as if by rote, "If I knew exactly what you were looking for?"

A voice behind me exclaimed, "Adrien, what are you doing here?"

I turned at this interruption to find Kevin standing there looking surprised and delighted all out of proportion to the circumstances. He wasn't the only one; Miss Buttermit's expression was close to beaming.

"Hey, Mitty," Kevin greeted her.

"Why, Kevin!"

I answered Kevin's question, glad to see that he was still at large, at least for the moment. "I'm trying to get access to the old newspapers in the basement."

"No problem," said Kevin. Then he caught Miss Buttermit's eye and looked guilty. "Oh. *Is* it a problem?"

"Apparently."

"Now, Kevin," Miss Buttermit cautioned. "You know there are channels."

"Yeah, but Adrien is…" Kevin seemed at a loss how to classify me. "How about this," he suggested suddenly, "I'll go downstairs with Adrien and take responsibility for the papers?"

I opened my mouth to say that wasn't necessary, but shut it again. Maybe it was necessary. I sure wasn't having any luck on my own. I watched Kevin work that hopeful puppy dog look for all it was worth.

"This is a *great* responsibility, Kevin," Miss Buttermit observed after a moment, but she took a key off her Mrs Danvers-like keyring and handed it over.

I followed Kevin past the water coolers and restrooms down two flights of stairs. Kevin unlocked the basement, and I stepped into a room as cold and smelly as the vegetable bin in a refrigerator, waiting till Kevin pulled the chain to turn on the ceiling bulb. Garish light bounced off faded green walls and a cement floor discoloured by water stains.

"Holy –" I didn't finish the sentence. I could barely finish the thought. There were filing cabinets, a few broken shelves, a chair minus a castor, but mostly there were books. We were surrounded by boxes and boxes and boxes of books.

"I think the newspapers are over on those metal shelves."

I stepped over a box of books stamped 'Discard,' steadying myself with one hand on the metal shelf stacked with hardbound volumes. The shelf wobbled alarmingly. "I wouldn't want to be here in an earthquake," I remarked.

"Nobody ever comes down here."

I opened the cover of the nearest book.

A glance verified that we were indeed looking at the earliest editions of *The Basking Gazette*.

"These aren't indexed," Kevin announced. "What are we looking for?"

"Any reference to the Red Rover mine."

He looked up interested, "Why's that?"

"It's just an idea." I studied Kevin. I liked him, but I respected Jake's opinion. Jake had a lot of experience when it came to bad guys. "Kevin, did Livingston call at all during the time he was supposed to be away from the dig?"

His jaw dropped. "He was *dead*," he reminded me.

"I know, but what I mean is, did anyone call saying they were Livingston? Or did anyone at the site claim to have heard from Livingston?"

Kevin had a weird expression. "Yeah," he said slowly. "He did call in – or at least we thought he did."

"Who took the calls?"

Kevin shook his head. "Amy? Marquez? I'm not sure. There were written messages a couple of times."

"Whose writing?"

"I'm not sure. No one questioned the notes." His eyebrows drew together. "Shoup seemed to be in contact with him. That's what we all thought anyway."

I tried another approach. "What's the deal with this mine? Why is everyone so interested in it?"

Kevin spluttered, "You're the one who wants to look through old newspapers. Don't you have a – a –"

"Plan?"

"No. A – a –" He gestured over his head.

"Theory?"

"Yeah, a theory. Do you honestly think one of us killed Livingston? Why? Because of some mine we couldn't even know we'd find?"

"Did anyone have any problem with Livingston? Anyone argue with him?"

"No. We all admired the man. We all *liked* him."

"Who didn't?"

"Nobody! He was…" Kevin shook his head. "He wasn't the kind of person who gets murdered."

"What do you mean?"

"He was a…a scholar and a gentleman. I guess that sounds corny. Archeology was his passion, but he loved teaching. He loved sharing his knowledge, and he made the past come alive. He made archeology a lot more than old bones and broken pottery."

I sat down in the broken chair which tilted drunkenly, and began to thumb through the pages of the volume I held.

After a moment Kevin pulled a volume off the shelf and sat down on a box across from me.

"Hey," he said after an hour of reading silently, "This is about the sinking of the *Titanic*. 'Mr Hubert Duke, a resident of Basking, was aboard the doomed vessel,'" he read aloud. "Pretty cool."

"Chilling." I glanced up. "When was the *Titanic?* 1912? You've got to go back a decade."

"Basking was founded in 1848."

"Royale came west in 1849. We're probably looking for something circa the 1850's. When did Royale die?"

"Beats me." Replacing one volume on the shelf, he pulled out another. "This could take forever," he muttered.

I was afraid he was right.

Another hour passed, and Miss Buttermit brought us coffee in Styrofoam cups and a plate of Fig Newtons.

"What's this mysterious hold you have over Miss Buttermit?" I asked Kevin, brushing crumbs off my hands.

"Hmm? Mitty? She's a sweetheart, isn't she? She's one of us."

"One of us?"

"Gay. Well, lesbian." He grinned at my expression. "She's not out or anything. People of her generation can't be."

"They can't?"

"Not in a small town."

I was still puzzling over that as Kevin lowered his gaze to the page before him. "Listen to this, Adrien. 'Abraham Royale dead at forty-five.' "

"What's the date?"

"September 11th 1860. Have you noticed, Adrien, that there are editions missing?"

"I was hoping it only seemed that way because they're not indexed."

"No, look how the dates jump around in this volume. It looks like someone tore out an edition."

I examined the volume. Sure enough it appeared someone had taken a razorblade to several pages.

"Where else might there be copies of this paper? The local college?"

Kevin shook his head. "I don't know. Maybe not everything was saved. Maybe some copies were lost or destroyed. This stuff is pretty fragile."

Gently I turned another yellowed page. History was literally turning to dust beneath my fingertips.

"These pages were here. They existed and someone removed them. Why?"

"It could have happened years ago, Adrien."

I took the volume from Kevin and scanned it. In brief, Abraham Royale had died after sustaining a head injury in a fall down his grand staircase. There had been no witnesses to the accident, and Royale had never regained consciousness. He was survived only by his estranged wife, Alicia Royale, *née* Salt.

"Salt." I looked up. "Where have I heard that name before?"

Kevin, his mouth full of Fig Newtons, shook his head.

" 'Estranged wife?' Weren't they divorced? She ran off with the blacksmith, didn't she?"

"Maybe he wouldn't give her a divorce," Kevin replied thickly. Jake was right, he did have freckles on his nose. Tiny, pale ones; kissable.

"Maybe. Maybe she pushed him. It sounds like he left a considerable fortune." I chewed my lip thoughtfully. "Salt! That's it. Barnabas Salt was the name of Royale's partner in the Red Rover mine. Alicia must have been his daughter." I considered this. "That must have made for some awkward moments around the sluice boxes."

"Salt was already dead by the time Royale married his daughter."

"How do you know?"

"It said so in the obit."

I continued reading. Kevin was correct. Salt had been killed a couple of years earlier in a shootout with Mexican bandits. "This would be interesting to read about," I said. "See if you can find the story of Salt's shootout with the *banditos*."

"It might be in one of the missing editions."

"It might not be."

We searched through the remaining volumes to no avail.

"Here's something," Kevin said, breaking another long silence. "A trapper was found mutilated in Senex Valley. Where the hell's Senex Valley?"

"Hmm? Senex Valley is what they used to call Spaniard's Hollow and the area surrounding it."

"When did they change the name?"

I answered absently, "I'm not really sure. It seems like it followed Salt's gun battle with the bandits."

"Spaniards aren't Mexicans."

"When you figure Mexico was still under Spanish rule as late as 1821, I think it's safe to assume some cultural overlay."

Silence broken only by the scrape of turning pages.

"This is pretty gruesome," Kevin commented, still glued to the *Gazette*.

I glanced at my watch. "Jesus! It's five o'clock!"

Kevin slapped shut the cover. "No wonder I'm starving." As I stood up he asked way too casually, "Can I buy you dinner?"

"No can do." I shoved the volume back on the shelf, held my hand out for Kevin's. "Besides, shouldn't you be getting back to camp?"

Kevin handed me the tome he held. "I've been asked to take a leave of absence until I'm cleared." The green eyes could not meet mine.

"Cleared?"

"Of Livingston's murder." His smile was bitter. "See, you're not the only one who thinks I'm capable of murder."

"Kev –"

"No, it's okay. I mean, why not me?"

"Because you didn't do it?"

"Do you believe that?"

Before I could answer, Kevin turned away. Turning out the light, he locked the door to the basement. As we started up the stairs he said, "I hear it was your friend who discovered Harvey's body."

"Uh, right." I had to wonder at the number of fibs my former Boy Scout was telling these days. Not that I didn't appreciate his running interference for me. I could imagine what the sheriff would have said if I'd discovered *another* body.

Over his shoulder Kevin asked, "What were you doing up in those caves? Were you looking for Harvey?"

"No." I tried to get my mind (and gaze) off the trim butt in the tight jeans moving at eye level as we continued back up the stairs. "Aren't the sheriffs questioning everybody?" I inquired.

"Sure, but they're just waiting for the damn ballistics match so they can arrest me."

We kept coming back to this. "Why should they think you killed Livingston?"

"I wouldn't have. I had no reason. He was a great guy."

"Somebody didn't think so."

"Then it was somebody who didn't know him."

I wished I could see his face as I asked, "Are you sure Livingston didn't argue with anyone? Were there any problems between

Livingston and Shoup?"

"No." He qualified, "Not that I know of."

"Do you know if Livingston ever met Ted Harvey?"

"I think he came around a couple of times when we first set up camp. There was never any confrontation."

Upstairs Kevin returned the key to Miss Buttermit's stand-in. As we walked outside into the spring evening he put a hand on my arm.

"Adrien, about yesterday…"

I laughed. "Forget it."

His fingers tightened. "I don't want to forget it." An internal struggle seemed to take place while the old-fashioned street lamps came on one by one around us. "It's not easy being gay in a town like Basking."

"It's not easy in a town like LA. It's not easy."

"I just wish –"

I almost said, 'me too,' which would have been a mistake, not least because it wasn't true.

Instead I gave his shoulder a little pat, got in my car and drove away leaving Kevin standing on the boardwalk in the shadow of a swinging sign in the shape of a boot.

I made a small detour on the drive home. Yesterday's exploration of the cave had not turned up exactly what I'd expected; that meant the proof I needed was still out there – and I thought I had a pretty good idea where.

An hour and a half later of crawling through bushes, climbing trees and sliding down hillsides, I wasn't quite so sure.

I was rethinking my brilliant plan as I rested on a flat-top rock formation overlooking the archeologist's strangely silent camp when I spotted some peculiar dents in the worn surface: pockets in the *metates* made by *manos*, or grinding stones, over decades. I knew I was on the right trail.

In fact…

I shifted my weary arse, hunting down among the weeds and supporting boulders, and sure enough, before the sun set, I had my proof in the form of the latest Japanese technology.

Not that it gave me any pleasure.

By the time I reached the ranch, it was nearly dark, the long muted shadows flecked with the smoke and heather tones of the mountains. Frederick Remington might have painted the sunset slashing the sky with Confederate blue and firebrand pink as I drove through the Pine Shadow gates. My headlamps picked out Jake striding purposefully across the yard, keys in hand. I parked and got out.

"Where the hell have you been?" From the drill sergeant bark, you'd have thought I'd overstayed my 24-hour pass. Then he added, "I was coming to look for you."

Well, that sounded kind of nice actually. It would have been nicer to have been kissed hello, but Jake stayed at arm's length

"I lost track of time." I still hadn't made up my mind what to do with the item in my jacket pocket, so I hedged.

"Doing what?"

"Looking through old newspapers." I debated whether to mention Kevin's presence, and decided that on *this* point, honesty *was* the best policy. "I ran into Kevin."

"Coincidence?" asked Jake. "I think not."

"I think so."

He followed me into the ranch house. I peeled off my jacket watching Jake shrug out of his own, wincing. I queried, "How's the arm?"

"Not so stiff." He lifted his shoulder like he was winding up to pitch a hardball. "Itches like hell. I think that's a good sign though."

"Not if it's infected. So what did you do today?"

"Made a few calls," Jake said vaguely.

That sort of clinched the quandary of fair exchange of information. "Oh yeah? What's to eat? All I've had since breakfast is coffee and cookies." I homed in on the kitchen where I discovered Jake had waiting grilled steaks and baked potatoes with all the trimmings.

"A man could get used to this," I remarked.

No comment from Jake.

While we ate, I filled him in on what I had learned. Jake listened impassively as though he sat on the opposite side of an interrogation table.

"Let me see if I understand you. You think something that happened over a hundred years ago connects the deaths of Harvey and Livingston?"

"I think it's possible."

"Uh huh." He chewed ferociously, swallowed and inquired, "What about the werewolf?"

"Laugh all you want, but there's something weird about this place. Do you know that over the past hundred-plus years over fifteen mutilated bodies have been found in the woods?"

"Do you know how many mutilated bodies have turned up in the Angeles Crest Forest over the past hundred years? Plenty."

"That's not a reasonable comparison, Jake. This is a small, relatively secluded area." I laid my fork and knife down. "They used to call this place Senex Valley. Senex is Latin for old. The old ones, the first ones... get it?"

Jake rubbed his forehead as though he felt a headache coming on.

"Maybe that's beside the point," I said hastily. "There's something about this Red Rover mine that isn't quite kosher."

"Like?"

"For starters, Royale and his partner Barnabas Salt abandoned the Red Rover. They thought it was worthless and they moved on. Then for some reason they came back to the mine and hit a vein."

"So?"

"That's not typical. It's practically unheard of."

"But it's possible, right?"

"Yes. But here's another bizarre thing. After Royale's death, they tried mining the Red Rover. The mine was played out."

"They who?" inquired Jake, getting down to brass tacks.

"I guess the ex-wife hired…"

"But you don't know."

"I don't know *who*, I do know efforts to mine the Red Rover after Royale's death failed. That's why the mine was abandoned and then finally lost track of."

"Which means something to you." Jake stroked the gold stubble on his lean jaw, as though noticing he needed a shave.

"I'm wondering why there was all this interest in a mine that played out so long ago?"

Jake pushed his plate aside and tilted his chair back, linking his hands behind his head.

"Like your pal, Shoup says, it's historically interesting, Adrien. You think only things of monetary value are of historical interest?"

"Of course not, but Marquez said something to the effect that Shoup would be interested in the mine because it would be a significant find. I just don't see how a played-out mine could be a significant find."

Jake cogitated. "It's hard to say, what with funding and grants and nutty professors in general."

"You don't think it's interesting?"

"I guess it's interesting." He shrugged.

By now we had finished eating. Stars twinkled through the windows. I rose and started piling dishes in the sink, wondering about our sleeping arrangements. Had last night been a one-off or had we been setting a precedent? Jake sat unmoving as I made my trips to and from the table. Other than a floorboard that squeaked every time I crossed it, the kitchen seemed uncannily quiet.

The four feet of his chair hit the floor with a bang and I nearly jumped out of my skin.

He raised his eyebrows. "What's with you?"

I shook my head sheepishly.

Jake grinned and shoved away from the table. "Let's leave the dishes," he suggested.

Like the song says, 'Don't try to understand 'em, just tie a rope and brand 'em.'

Sober, it was different: slower, sweeter. Jake explored my body with a thoroughness that would lead one to think he was doing a comparison check, inspecting what wasn't there, inspecting what was. He tried a couple of things, watching my face to see how I took it – and I took it like a man, encouraging him as best I could without making him self-conscious. What he lacked in technique he made up for in enthusiasm. When we were worn out playing, Jake pulled me against him, gave my rump a friendly little pat and plunged into sleep.

I followed a few minutes after.

When I woke it was several hours later. The room was illuminated by moonlight. I lay there for a moment or two wondering at the sound that had dispersed my dreams.

I rose up on my elbow, listening. "Did you hear that?" I whispered.

Had I really heard that eerie howling or had it been part of my uneasy dreams? A ringing silence met my ears.

Jake made a sound between a snore and a grunt, and rolled on to his side. A werewolf would have to actually be hopping up and down on the foot of the bed for him to notice.

I settled back in the blankets, resting my head against Jake's back. His bare skin was warm and smooth against my face. Comforting. I kissed him beneath his shoulder blade.

Sex wasn't everything. There were other things: someone to see you through sickness and in health, someone to wake up with on Christmas morning, someone to bail you out of jail. Companionship counted. Sex wasn't everything – but it was a lot.

Jake began snoring.

Thirteen

"Marnie Starr has an alibi for the night Ted Harvey was killed," Jake informed me over eggs and bacon the next morning.

"Oh? Oh."

Correctly interpreting my lack of enthusiasm, Jake said, "I know you already knew your second DB was Harvey. And I know you have your heart set on lost gold mines and ghostly assassins, but it never hurts to answer the easy questions first."

I ignored the jibe. "So what's her alibi?"

"Ms Starr was playing bingo. At least ten people will testify she was at the Moose Club all night, eventually walking away with a lovely Chia pet." Jake splashed more coffee into my cup and then his own. "Your boy Kevin does not have an alibi."

I wondered why he had not shared this information last night? Didn't want to ruin the mood? "Does everyone else at the camp have an alibi?"

"Shoup and Marquez were going over grid maps or something."

"At midnight?"

"That's their story. There's no reason to doubt it. Pocahontas was staying with friends in Sonora. O'Reilly and what's-her-name-Bernice were sleeping in camp – not together, so it doesn't count towards an alibi. The girl, Amy, took the first watch, and allegedly hit the sack afterwards."

"So no one has an alibi except Marquez and Shoup. So that really doesn't mean anything."

"It's not conclusive."

"What about the autopsy results? Lab tests? Ballistics?"

"As of yesterday, Billingsly hadn't got the ballistics report. The autopsy confirmed Harvey was the corpse in the cave; that he was most likely killed Thursday night or early Friday morning; and tentatively, that he was killed by the same weapon that killed Livingston, most likely a .22 hollow-point."

"Why is this taking so long?"

Jake raised his eyebrows. "It's not taking 'so long.' This isn't TV with a fifteen-minute crime lab turnaround. Lab results take a day or two. Figure in that this is a small town and a not particularly... urgent... case."

"Have they confirmed that Kevin's rifle was used?"

Jake's honey-coloured eyes met mine. "They haven't confirmed it, but the kid's rifle had been fired recently and the load is right. It was his gun all right."

"He keeps that rifle in a gun rack in his truck. Anyone could have borrowed it."

"You're assuming premeditation?"

"Yes, definitely. First Livingston is murdered and hidden in the barn. Why?" I answered my own question. "Because someone wanted to hide the fact that he was dead. His car was parked in town so that everyone would think he'd gone to San Francisco as planned. And if his body *were* to be discovered, it would implicate Harvey."

"Harvey *is* implicated. His being dead cinches that." Jake swallowed a mouthful of coffee. "Do you have any idea of the street value of an acre of marijuana?"

I applied the little grey cells. "You'd have to be able to process and market it. It would depend on the grade... and the particular street."

"Taking all that into consideration, do you have a rough notion of what that cash crop was worth?"

"No."

Jake's mouth quirked. "At last estimate a pound of cannabis was valued between $700-900. An acre could bring in anywhere from $50,000 to a cool million. Now, do you still think that pot was not a motive?"

That shook my certainty, I had to admit. "It's not the only possible motive, surely?"

"No, but it's the most likely." He reached into the pocket of his flannel shirt and set a misshapen bit of metal next to the pepper shaker. "I dug this out of your front porch post. It's a 30.6."

As I suspected, the reason he had been so accommodating about my library research was he intended to do the real sleuthing while my back was turned. "So someone else shot at us?"

"Or the same perp used a different gun."

"Because they couldn't get access to Kevin's?"

Jake sighed.

"You tell me what you think happened," I invited cordially, picking up my coffee cup.

"I don't know what happened. I can guess. Harvey arranged for a buyer. Someone with connections, maybe a student at a local college. Livingston found out about it, made threats. This unknown person eliminates Livingston. Maybe he tries to frame Harvey for it by planting Livingston in the barn here. It's clear Harvey and his confederate had some kind of falling out because Harvey was iced five days later."

It was a neat fit. Logical. Absently, I scratched the yellow jacket bite on my hand. Looking down at the red welt, a tiny memory flickered in the back of my mind.

Jake's next words derailed my train of thought. "From everything I've been able to find out, Livingston sounds like an up and up guy. Strict but fair; I heard that about three times. The worst anyone could say was he lacked imagination."

"Who said that?"

"Dr Shoup."

"Did you do any background checking on Shoup while you were at it?"

Jake studied my face as though he couldn't read my tone. "Yeah, I did some checking. Apparently there was some problem between him and the British Museum. A question of selling antiquities."

I opened my mouth but Jake said flatly, "Nothing was proved, but he was asked to resign, and he did. His problems at Berkley have to do with a salary dispute. From what I gathered, he felt he was worth a lot more than he was being paid."

"*Selling antiquities?* And you don't think there's a tie in?"

"What antiquities were sold or even stolen here?"

"Jake, the man was suspected of –"

He cut me off cold. "Baby, you were suspected of murder once, remember? Were you guilty?"

"No, but don't you think it's too much coincidence –"

"Don't you think the sheriff thinks it's too much coincidence that now you're involved in a second homicide case?"

I didn't have an answer. At last I grumbled, "What about Marquez?"

"There's nothing on Marquez. He had a parking ticket about ten years ago." Jake said, more kindly than I was used to from him, "Let's go home, Adrien. I'm running out of vacation and you're not going to enjoy the next few days."

I stared at him: the pale, sleep-mussed hair, the leonine eyes that could unexpectedly warm with amusement, the firm mouth that tasted uniquely Jake. What could I say? Maybe our relationship was undefined, but he had proven his friendship a dozen times over the past week. He had come to my rescue without being asked, he had spent his vacation making sure I didn't get myself killed playing detective; hell, he had taken a bullet that could have been meant for me. Gay or straight, I never had a better friend. Now he was asking me for something, asking probably as much for my sake as his own. I listened to the water dripping from the leaky tap to the sink in slow, regretful tears. I nodded.

I had the best intentions. I intended to go straight to the realtor's office and arrange for someone to stay at the ranch as a caretaker, but somehow I found myself driving past the library one last time.

When Miss Buttermit saw me coming she made a fluttery gesture – like a villager warding off the Evil Eye.

"I was hoping..." I began.

Miss Buttermit whipped the key off her key ring and handed it over with conspiratorial haste. I thanked her and returned once more to the basement.

Though pressed for time, I now thought I knew what I was looking for. And after some feverish page turning, I found it. In 1857 a stagecoach travelling from Basking to Sonora had been robbed by three Mexican bandits. The stagecoach had been carrying an unusual load: gold from local mines bound for San Francisco. Valued at well over three million dollars, the hold-up had taken place in Senex Valley, not long after the stage left the stage stop. The two guards riding shotgun had been killed, the driver wounded.

I was absently scratching the yellow jacket bite on my hand when I read this and, as I stared down at the welt, a little pink light bulb went off. Granted, it was an idea that probably should have lit the echoing corridors of my empty brain before now. The first clue had been right under my eyes that very first day.

Hurriedly I hunted through the shelves, pouring through every volume, scanning every page, but I could find nothing more about the stagecoach robbery.

Taking the stairs two at a time, I cornered Miss Buttermit about the missing newspapers.

Miss B seemed to be mostly concerned with the defacement of library property, but at last I got her to focus on my question.

"You!" she answered indignantly. "You and Kevin were the last ones to examine those papers." She looked mad enough to revoke my library card on the spot.

"Anyone else? Anyone from the archeological site?"

Miss Buttermit thought back and shook her head. "It was weeks ago. It couldn't have been *him*."

"Him who?"

"The doctor. The English doctor."

"Dr. Shoup?"

"The very man," concurred Miss Buttermit.

Taking Miss Buttermit's advice, I left the library and cut across to Royale House. An urgency close to panic nipped at my heels.

I caught Melissa on the porch, locking the front doors. CLOSED, read the sign swinging inside the glass pane.

"I can't talk now," she told me, whipping past me on the stairs. The tips of her black hair floated against my face and I thought of the story she had told me of Royale's first wife.

"Hold on." I caught her arm. "Are there copies of the *Basking Gazette* archived here?"

She scowled. "Why?"

"Because the library doesn't have a complete set and I need to check something out."

"Can't it wait? Kevin's been arrested and the dig's been called off. Hadn't you heard?"

"No." My fingers tightened on her arm as she started to pull away.

Impatiently she said, "They matched the bullets that killed Harvey and Livingston to Kevin's rifle."

Jake had hinted that was coming, but it was still a shock.

"I don't believe it," I said automatically.

"It's a fact. They found traces of blood and hair in Kevin's truck bed. They think he used the pickup to transport the bodies." Her black eyes held mine. "But you know all this."

"I do?"

"Sure. You and your copper pal have been working with the sheriff."

"We have?"

"Don't play dumb." She smiled. I'd never noticed what sharp little incisors she had. "What were you up to, wandering around in those caves above the hollow, if you weren't looking for Harvey's body?"

She was a pretty woman, but more than prettiness there was strength and character in the face turned to mine. I didn't understand her, but I admired her in a way.

"I think you know what I was looking for Melissa," I said gently.

After a moment red suffused her dusky skin. "I don't know what you're talking about," she said.

"I'm talking about spirit voices echoing out of the caves at night when all good little archeologists are tucked snug in their sleeping bags. I'm talking battery-operated Kuksu in stereophonic sound."

She went very still, didn't move a muscle. A hell of a poker player she'd make.

I said, "Are you going to let me in the museum or not?"

She pivoted on her heels, marched back up the stairs and unlocked the frosted glass paned door.

"Do you have proof?" she asked, her back to me.

"Yes, I think so." Instinctively I patted the pocket of my denim jacket.

As we stepped into the museum she said, "I didn't kill anyone."

"But you know who did."

She did face me then. "No, I don't! If I did, do you think I'd let them arrest O'Reilly?"

"Truthfully? I don't know."

"Well, I wouldn't! The guy's a pain, but..."

"Then what's up with the sabotage? Are you saying you haven't been trying to stop the dig?"

"NO ONE HAS BEEN HURT!" She yelled it so loudly I expected the portrait of the giant-sized Abraham Royale to blink.

"What about the dog?" I was beginning to feel like Sherlock Holmes in *Silver Blaze*, forever going on about the curious incident of the dog in the night-time.

"What about the damned dog? Coyotes got it." Yet something about her expression didn't seem what it ought.

I thought, *she believes in the legend of the Guardian.*

More calmly Melissa said, "I don't expect you to understand."

"Try me."

She said nothing. A born martyr looking forward to the first burning brand.

I said, "You took over your grandfather's shaman duties, didn't you? You've said a number of times you believe the hollow is sacred."

"Oh for – ! *Life* is sacred," Melissa retorted. "I wanted to stop the desecration of holy ground, but I wouldn't kill anyone to do it."

"Did you put a snake in my mailbox?"

"Did I what?" Her mouth dropped. "Are you kidding me?"

I tended to believe her – or her expression anyway.

"Can I check the newspaper archives?"

Melissa checked her watch. I checked mine. I'd promised Jake I'd be back within the hour, and forty-five minutes had passed already.

"I don't have time for this. The Student Union has asked me to organise legal aid for O'Reilly," she said. "I've got things to do and people to see."

"If we can prove who really killed Livingston and Harvey, legal aid won't be necessary."

Undecided, she contemplated me and then turned with a whirl of her black hair and led the way downstairs.

The cellar of Royale House was cool and dry. Melissa lit a lantern and the smell of kerosene mingled with the smell of dried apples and sawdust.

"What year are we looking for?" She inquired, dragging out a bulging cardboard box. I moved to help her.

"1857, I think. Something to do with a gun battle between Mexican bandits. Royale's partner, Barnabas Salt was killed."

"I know about that," Melissa said. "The same *banditos* had robbed the stage a couple of weeks before. They got away with a couple million dollars worth of gold dust and bullion."

"Everybody in the county must have been hunting them."

"Yep, but Salt and Royale found them holed up in Senex Valley."

"And in the ensuing fight, the bandits and Salt were killed."

"'Ensuing fight'," mocked Melissa. "I could listen to you for hours. Do you write like you talk?"

"You wouldn't want to concentrate here, would you?"

"In the *ensuing* fight," Melissa informed me, "all three bandits were shot to pieces, along with good old Barnabas Salt."

"And was the gold recovered?"

Her expression went totally blank.

"Yoo-hoo," I prompted. "The ill-gotten gains: whatever happened to them?"

She snapped back into life. "Never mind that box." She disappeared into a dusty recess and reappeared dragging another box over. The friction of the stone floor tore the deteriorating box apart. Newspapers spilled everywhere. "Fuck! Try these. This is the time frame we're interested in."

Evelyn Wood couldn't have speed-read any faster through those brittle, yellowed pages. The kerosene lamp threw flickering shadows that danced against the wall like Zuni spirit helper figures. I kept watching them out of the corner of my eye.

"Try to be careful, can't you? These are historically valuable."

"*I* am being careful." I nodded pointedly as a piece of page broke off in her hand. It was just like old times. "Maybe we should get some help."

"There's no time. He knows how close we are. He's liable to split any minute."

He. We both knew now who we were after but neither of us had put it in words yet.

"Without the gold?"

"Maybe he's found the gold."

Maybe. Maybe not. What was it about gold that drove men to leave their homes and families, to risk everything – to commit murder – on just the promise of it. Gold fever, they called it back then. In the 1800s it had been an epidemic; now and then there was still an outbreak.

"What happens if we can't find anything?" Melissa asked after a silence of some time.

"I don't know. I don't know that finding the right article will help. We have to use that information to confront him."

"You think he's going to fall apart because we shove an old newspaper article in his face? We've got to do more than that."

I should have listened to her, but my attention was caught by the article before me.

BANDITS SLAIN IN SHOOT OUT proclaimed the banner headline. In the faded old-fashioned typescript I read how Abraham Royale and Barnabas Salt had been set upon by the three notorious Mexican bandits who had robbed the Sonora stagecoach line only days before. A gun battle had ensued (that word again), and all three miscreants had been slain, saving the honest taxpayers of Calavares County the expense of hanging Juan Martinez, Eduardo Marquez, and Luis Quintana. Tragically, Barnabas Salt, Royale's long time partner in the Red Rover mine, had also been killed. The search for the stolen booty continued.

I lowered the paper. A moth was bumping against the lantern, a soft desperate sound as it fought to immolate itself. Melissa stared at my face and then eased the paper out of my hands.

While she read I worked it out. The bandits had hidden their loot in an abandoned mine, but the mine's previous owners, working nearby, had spotted them, or somehow become suspicious. There was a fight and everyone ended up dead except for one man. One man who chose to keep the hard-earned gold of his neighbors and friends for himself.

"What should we do?" Melissa asked when she finished reading.

"I think it's time to call the cops."

"The cops!" She looked outraged. "You said yourself this isn't proof. The last thing we need is Barney Fife stumbling around in this."

"Melissa, there's enough here to give them a start. It implicates someone other than Kevin."

"We don't need the cops for this!"

My nerves on edge, I snapped back, "For what? What did you have in mind? A citizen's arrest? He's killed two people so far."

"Your buddy Riordan –"

"Don't drag Jake into this."

She lowered he head, her hair falling across her face in a veil. She murmured, "Okay, you win. I'll call the cops from upstairs." Then she stood, backed up and ran for the stairs, shooting up the rickety staircase like a scalded cat.

A moment later the door to the cellar banged shut.

It took a nanosecond for the full implication of the sound of a slamming door – and the sound that followed: a key turning in a lock – to register.

I rocketed up the stairs in her wake yelling Melissa's name with all the sound and fury I could muster. As I reached the top step she called through the wood, "Just be grateful it's not a fruit cellar!"

"Open the goddamn door!" I pounded my fist on the door. Solid oak; it was like punching stone. I wasn't getting out that way, not without a Roman legion at my back. "Melissa, don't be stupid. *Melissa!*" I rattled the doorknob.

The sound of her footsteps died away.

I ran back down the stairs, which shook under the force of my feet. A quick scan of the cellar didn't offer much in the way of escape routes. There was no other door. There were a couple of small rectangular windows about ten feet up, probably street level.

Looking around for something to stand on, I spotted a trunk in the wavering lantern light. With some shoving and tugging, I got the trunk positioned beneath one of the windows. I hopped on top of it and found myself still about two feet too short.

I jumped down, searched around the corners disturbing the spiders in their webs, and came up with a milk bottle crate. I placed the crate on the trunk and gingerly climbed back up. The crate wobbled crazily on the curved lid of the trunk. Crouched, I balanced like a surfer, stood up slowly and rested my hand on the window sill.

Wiping a swath with my fist, I stared through the dirty window. I could see the street bathed in sunshine and the tyres of cars whizzing past. I pried at the rusty latch.

No good. The damn thing could have been welded shut.

I was mad enough to punch through the window, but not stupid enough. I needed something that wasn't my fist to break through the glass. A sledgehammer would be good, but that was too much to hope for. What kind of cellar didn't have a handy crowbar or even a broom?

I was thinking about taking my shirt off and wrapping it around my hand when a face loomed into the window, one eye blinking through the circle of clean.

I nearly fell off my perch. When I had steadied myself and looked again, the face was gone from the window.

"Hey!" I shouted. "Help!"

Leaping down, I unbuttoned my shirt, swathed it around my hand and clambered back up. The crate rocked and I teetered like Gidget Goes Beserk. Trying to stabilize my weight, with one hand I clutched the window sill and with the other I feinted cautiously at the glass. With the second punch my fist shattered the pane. Most of the glass flew streetward, the rest of it dusted my face and shoulders. I shook my head, blinking carefully. Wiping the glass out of the window frame, I rested both hands on the sill and hauled myself up.

Though it looks easy enough in movies, it ain't so easy in real life, to pull yourself up and wriggle through a small square window. With some writhing and squirming and a lot of swearing I managed to scrape through the window and crawl out to the sidewalk.

"You are an abomination and shall be put to death, your blood upon your head," the Reverend John Howdy shrieked into my sweating face.

I blinked up at him, and decided that all my parts were in working order.

"How's that?" I huffed. He proceeded to tell me how. When I had my wind back, I sat up, brushing off the glass and cobwebs.

"You – you!" he spluttered.

I ducked back from the fiery breath of the little man bending over me.

"Breaking and entering, you buggering spawn of Satan," he cried. "I'm calling the police!"

"Breaking and exiting," I retorted, getting to my knees. "And calling the police is a good idea. Send them to Pine Shadow ranch."

I could hear him hollering for the law as I limped off down the street.

There was no sign of Jake at the ranch. His car was packed with his gear; my suitcases were packed and sitting just inside the door. He was dead serious about our leaving on schedule. Mobilization had begun.

Dust covers blanketed the furniture once more, the shutters were closed and fastened, the thermostat was off, the fridge was empty.

"Jake!" I called, walking through the silent rooms.

There was no answer. Something felt wrong.

"Jake?" I heard the note of panic in my voice, and clamped down on it hard.

Walking out on the porch, I froze mid-step at the distant crack of two gun shots.

It could have been hunters, but I knew it wasn't, and can't quite describe the sick chill that spread from my gut to my heart.

"He's not dead," I said aloud.

Nothing contradicted me. The cowbell chimes stirred softly in the breeze.

I turned and went back inside to call the sheriffs. I don't think I really heard what the person on the other end of the line said. I was probably instructed to stay put, but the moment I hung up, I climbed the hillside behind the house, jogging past the scorched marijuana field, shearing through the trees, and slipping and sliding down the pine needles of the mountainside overlooking the camp in Spaniard's Hollow.

Or rather, where the camp had been. The kind of mass exodus that generally precedes the appearance of giant ants seemed to have taken place. I prowled the mauled grounds. Giant yellow squares indicated where the tents formerly sat, but the tents and the generators were gone, and the only vehicles parked by the tarn were Melissa's white pickup, a Land Rover and another car. I figured the Land Rover was probably Shoup's, since he lay face up beside it.

'The very man,' Miss Buttermit had said. I had thought at the time that he must be in on it too, but now I wondered.

I squatted down beside Shoup's body, and felt his throat for a pulse.

Even dead, he had a supercilious expression at odds with the wound in his chest.

I guess you do eventually get hardened to violent death, or else

I was too worried about Jake to feel much of anything for anyone else.

Shoup was stone-cold, so the shots I'd heard had not been the ones that had done him in. Rising to my feet I squinted at the sun glittering on the tarn, the dazzle stinging my eyes.

Why would he come back here? We were supposed to be getting the hell out of Dodge; why would Jake head back to the camp? It was so typical of that beef-witted lout to go off half-cocked, thinking he had all the answers when he only knew part of the story...

After a despairing couple of moments it occurred to me where they must have gone. Now I had another choice to make. I could wait for the sheriffs; I could follow them down the stagecoach tracks; or I could try to beat them to the Red Rover mine by cutting across the mountainside. The wrong decision could cost Jake's life.

If he wasn't dead already.

I went bounding back up the mountainside, my shoes slipping over stones and dried grass without regard to my neck or heart. Hell, I figured if my pump hadn't given out by now, it was probably good for the duration. Just so long as it saw me through getting Jake back in one piece; that was the bargain I was offering God.

By now I had worked out most of the details, like why Livingston, who everyone agreed was as straight and true as the needle on a compass, had to die the minute he got wise to what was happening at the site.

As for my former caretaker, Harvey must have been playing how-does-your-garden-grow on the mountainside and seen Livingston shot. Ever a lad with his eye to the main chance, he must have tried to cut a deal. My guess was he had threatened blackmail, probably claiming he held some incriminating evidence, like photos, which was why his trailer had been searched a couple of times. I suspected there never *was* any evidence but, either way, the blackmail scheme had backfired. Livingston's body had been planted in the barn to incriminate Harvey, and Harvey himself had been killed and dragged off to look like he'd rabbited.

While I climbed, I was thinking long and hard. What happened when I did catch them up? I didn't have a gun, and I didn't have a plan, and the force of my personality was not going to get us far.

I stepped wrong and went down on my knees. As I knelt there, panting and perspiring, I heard a sound. A minor explosion that resembled...a sneeze.

My heart lit and soared like a Roman candle; I'd recognise those tormented sinuses anywhere. I crawled over and peered through the bushes. And sure enough, a few moments later I glimpsed the top of three heads through the trees branches shading the trail below; Jake's gilt hair shone like a knight's helmet. He was alive.

I crawled forward as quietly as possible. Melissa was walking on Jake's right; Marquez followed close – though not too close – behind. He carried a rifle aimed at their backs. I'd have bet money on a 30.6 load.

"Hurry it up," Marquez's voice carried.

I didn't envy his task; even from my hiding place it was clear from their rigid body language, that Jake and Melissa were waiting for the first opportunity to turn on their captor. Marquez knew it too, if his strained white face was anything to go by.

How the hell had both Jake and Melissa managed to fall into Marquez's clutches? But wasn't it just typical of these damned 'A' personality heroic types, always thinking they knew best, always thinking they could handle whatever cropped up?

On hands and knees, I slunk forward. I had to get ahead of them. It was our only chance. But if I stood up, Marquez would spot me and probably start shooting. He was scared and desperate, so there was no predicting.

And in the clear mountain air even the sound of a snapping branch seemed to carry a mile. I could go back and wait for the sheriffs. It was probably the smartest thing to do. It was obviously the safest – and I was sure it was what Jake would have wanted me to do. I also knew it was not what Jake would have done were our positions reversed.

I moved the branches aside, listening tautly.

Reassuringly, Jake's voice floated up. He sounded calm, even conversational. "You don't actually have the gold then? You just think you know where it is."

"It's there."

"It's been over a hundred years, pal. Anything could have happened to it."

"If someone else had found it, it would have made history. Royale's wife didn't find it; she died in poverty."

"That's my point," Jake said. He was doing the cop thing: keep 'em talking; it distracts them and builds a bond whether the bad guy wants it or not. "If the gold was there someone would have found it before now."

"Before my great great-grandfather was murdered by Royale and Salt, he sent my grandmother a letter saying the gold was hidden in the mine."

A little knowledge is a dangerous thing, I recalled Dr Shoup saying only a few days earlier. How right he had been.

"Royale could have moved the gold before he died," Melissa said scornfully. "Which means you've killed two people for nothing."

"Shut up and walk!" Marquez sounded harassed. Clearly he was making it up as he went. What had gone wrong, I wondered?

The bushes were thinning. Dropping to my belly, I made like

G I Joe, creeping along over the hard ground. This is another thing that looks a lot easier in the movies than it is in real life. In real life dragging yourself over rock ground without making a sound is a slow and painful business. And as quiet and careful as I was being, I was still afraid they could hear the shift and slide of stones, the snap of twigs. I could hear them. But slowly, surely, I had gradually pulled ahead of the trio in the road below. A few more yards of this and it would be safe to stand again. The shinnying along on elbows was painful; my hips felt bruised.

Suddenly it occurred to me why it was so painful: I still had Melissa's cassette player in my pocket.

As this realisation sunk into my tired brain, I felt a spark of hope. Vigour renewed, I humped along, scraping myself raw over rocks and pine cones and tree roots.

The voices behind me faded. Scrambling to my feet, I ran like hell across the hillside, and then down through the trees.

I reached the mine a scant two minutes before they walked into view down the track. There was just time to prop the cassette player in the 'V' of a pine branch. I pressed play and slid up the volume, praying the recorder didn't fall off its perch. Up close the chanting sounded so obviously synthetic, I couldn't imagine how it had fooled anyone, but as I moved away from the sound, it got a little creepier. A little more believable.

I inched down the hillside, hiding behind a thicket, sweating and shaking.

It didn't take long before I heard their voices.

"So if Shoup was working with you, why kill him?" Jake was saying reasonably. As they drew even with my hiding place I could see Jake's eyes raking the hillside, the road, looking for his chance. For a sec, his eyes seemed to find mine in the thicket I hid in, but his expression never changed.

There was a bruise darkening his forehead, but he was okay. He was alive and on his feet and I planned on him staying that way. I felt around on the ground for a tree limb long and thick enough to use as a club.

"Because he finally figured out I-I disposed of Dan – Dr Livingston. And that scumball, Harvey."

"Disposed of? You mean kill?"

Melissa said, "You mean murdered? Because that's what it was. Cold-blooded murder, you bastard."

"Shut up!" Marquez shouted.

"Yeah, shut up," Jake growled. "You'll hurt his feelings."

Melissa stopped walking. "Do you hear that?" Her head jerked from side to side in disbelief. "What is that?"

About time, too. I was beginning to think the three of them would never shut up long enough to hear the ghostly voices soughing on the afternoon wind.

"That's enough!" bit out Marquez, his pale face glistening, his glasses shining like insect eyes in the sunlight.

"I hear it too," Jake said.

"It's the goddamn wind!" Marquez shoved at Melissa with the rifle barrel. She fell to her knees in the road and put her hands to her face. Jake wheeled to face Marquez.

I thought Marquez would blast them then and there, and I stood up.

Jake didn't charge though, instead he said, "Listen! Hear 'em? Sirens."

Sure enough, the distant wail of sirens could be heard echoing through the mountains.

"Bullshit! Hurry up, get in there!" Thoroughly rattled, Marquez tried to nudge Melissa to her feet with the rifle barrel. She wasn't cooperating and I didn't blame her. If he got them inside the mine they'd never walk out alive.

Keeping a wary eye on Jake, Marquez poked at her with the rifle. Suddenly Melissa surged to her feet, swaying a little, wheeling to face Marquez. Marquez gasped and stepped back from her, the gun shaking wildly.

The unnerving thing was, Jake *also* stepped back from her.

He was blocking my view of Melissa, but I could see Marquez's face and I thought, *it's now or never.* Sucking in a deep breath, I bellowed over the taped chanting – and the distant cry of approaching sirens, "Police! Drop your weapon!"

Marquez swung the rifle my way and both Melissa and Jake jumped him.

Things got a little confused at that point, like one of those cartoon fights where all you see is a giant ball of dust and the occasional fist or foot. Jake was wrestling for the rifle, which fired once into the sky and once into the forest before Jake wrested it away from Marquez. All the while Melissa was howling like a war chief right out of cowboy cinema, clawing and kicking anybody she could reach.

I circled the action, trying to see how to help without getting in the way or getting shot. Catching sight of Melissa's snarling face, I got the shock of my life. Her eyes were glowing red like something out of *The Exorcist.*

Having wrenched the rifle free, Jake staggered to his feet. "Get up," he ordered Marquez. He spared me a look. "Adrien, don't step between him and the gun."

I tore my eyes away from Melissa's demonic gaze. Marquez, his glasses hanging from his ears, his nose bloody, dived towards the mine entrance.

"Halt!" Jake yelled.

I don't think he could hear Jake over Melissa's yells. Jake fired into the timber frame. Undeterred, Marquez wriggled though the wooden slats still half-covering the mouth of the mine and disappeared inside.

"God damn it!" Jake swore.

We raced for the entrance.

From inside the mine Marquez screamed hysterically, a full-throated, sharp blood-curdling shriek straight out of Edgar Allen Poe that tailed and then abruptly cut off.

The silence that followed was more terrible than that dying scream.

Jake and I stared at each other, and then Jake started to climb through the boards. "No, wait!" Melissa cried as we both grabbed for him.

"Are you nuts?" I shouted, locking my arms around him. "The stairs are gone!"

"He's fallen down the mine shaft!" Melissa said. Her face was blanched of colour, her eyes... they were still glowing. Hastily, I looked away.

Jake was staring at us like we were speaking in tongues, and then to my utter amazement, he pulled me against him in a rough embrace that nearly knocked the wind out of me.

"I owe you one, baby," he muttered against my ear. I could feel his heart banging away with exertion and excitement against my own. It was the most beautiful sound in the world, and I closed my eyes as I listened and thought, *I love you.*

It was old news, really. I guess I'd been in love with him since I left LA. I guess that was why I'd left LA, because there wasn't any future in it. Not really. The things I wanted from life – and Jake – weren't things he could give. But somehow at that moment it just didn't matter.

I barely heard Melissa babbling, "He must have forgotten that the stairs had rotted away. I know we told him. Kevin and I noticed when we were out here. Only the top two rungs are left. I know we told him. He... must have forgotten."

"He knew," I told her.

Jake's arms tightened around me like he was picturing himself tumbling down the shaft on Marquez's heels. "Poor bastard," he muttered against my ear.

I nodded. I honest-to-God couldn't find my voice, too choked with idiot emotion when I least needed it.

"No one could survive that fall," Melissa said, though no one was really listening. "He's dead. He must be. Maybe he meant to do it all along. Maybe..."

The sirens were close now, wailing through the trees like electronic banshees. As the first car appeared on the road, Jake released me and stepped back. He massaged the back of his neck self-consciously.

"He must be dead," Melissa repeated. "Don't you think?"

"Yeah," I said.

Somehow the sun was already setting again. It was going to be another cold night. I rubbed my nose hard. "What happened?" I asked Jake. "Why the hell did you come back here?" I stopped as colour flooded his face.

"I had a bad feeling," he said. "You gave in too easily this morning. I know you – well, I thought I did. I started thinking you were going to come back here and do something... dumb."

"Dumb?"

"Like in a book. You know, gather all the suspects in the drawing room and try to trick the murderer into confessing."

"So you did something dumb instead?"

The clearing was suddenly full of cop cars and uniforms. The sound of voices and slamming car doors carried in the late afternoon.

Jake said, "I... er..." He cleared his throat. "I was just in the wrong place at the wrong time. Shoup confronted Marquez. He was waving this old newspaper in his face. Then Marquez popped Shoup. That's when she showed up." He glanced at Melissa, doing a double-take at her flaming red orbs, and breaking off what he was saying to exclaim, "And lady, what is with *you?*"

Melissa met our gazes blankly. Then she gave a weak laugh, and popped out the trick eyeballs.

Sharing can be murder

The Lodger
by Drew Gummerson

Honza takes in a lodger, Andy, who seems like his opposite – a coarse straight guy who comes home drunk every night to fart happily in front of the TV. But when, in a drunken stupor, Andy confesses to murder, Honza refuses to believe him. Then one weekend Andy disappears, only to return with his face rearranged.

A black comedy of misunderstandings, *The Lodger* is a modern, engaging debut written in an easy, witty style.

UK £9.99 US $13.95 (when ordering direct, quote LOD400)